Life and Law

The Steamship Chronicles
Book Four

Margaret McGaffey Fisk

TTO
PUBLISHING

Visit the author at:

Website: margaretmcgaffeyfisk.com
Twitter: @Marfisk
Facebook: MargaretMcGaffeyFisk

Praise for the Books of Margaret McGaffey Fisk

Secrets

"Through her young heroine and hero, the author breathes life into a curious, exciting and often dangerous world of steam, sail, sentient machines, loyal friendships and deeds of quiet bravery undertaken in the face of widespread fear and bigotry, to deliver a clever, entertaining and unique new take on Victorian Steampunk."
— David Bridger, author of *A Flight of Thieves (Sky Ships)* —

Shafter

"Trina's life revolves around protecting her family and as a shafter, the lowest of Ceric society, her choices are limited to what she can steal. However, a chance at a new life aboard a colony-bound ship teaches her a new way of life and the price of unquestioned loyalty in this exciting tale, rich with cultural world building and science fiction adventure. This is a story you'll love, with a tale you won't want to see end!"
— Lazette Gifford, author of *Glory* —

"While the heroine yearns for another world, you'll crave any universe, any tale, created by this exciting new speculative fiction author. In Shafter, McGaffey Fisk delivers an inter-planetary colony system and populates it with complex and sympathetic characters. Travel from the tunnels of Ceric to the stars beyond with a master thief and her master storyteller."
— Valerie Comer, author of *Majai's Fury* —

1

enry held Lily nestled beside him on the sitting room couch. Her head lay pillowed against his shoulder and her feet were tucked under her as she'd scolded Sam for many a time. He stroked her soft blond hair, spinning out yet another tale of where her little sister would be at this very moment though Lily had fallen into a doze.

"It's been two days. She should have reached the village by now. Stuart would have sent my letter ahead. A representative from the safe haven will be waiting for them, waiting to bring her to a place where she will finally find the freedom you always wanted for her."

He told Lily nothing he had not said before, and she couldn't hear him anyway, but Henry found as much comfort as his wife did in the knowledge that Sam had found a place of happiness at last.

He missed her more than he would have thought possible, his parents' estate a solemn place without Sam's laughter and cheeky mischief to brighten it. The servants felt much the same, going about with mournful expressions as though someone had died.

All except Kate.

If that young woman hadn't been a help and comfort to Lily from the moment Henry brought them here from London, he'd have sent the maid packing to her father's house in the village just to rid himself of the sight of her smile.

As though fate laughed at him, a quick knock at the open door revealed Kate just then.

Henry shook his head, tipping it toward his sleeping wife.

When the lady's maid stepped to one side to reveal none other than Stuart, his man from Dover, Henry couldn't hold back a curse.

Lily stirred against his shoulder, her head lifting free a moment later as she blinked awake. "Henry?"

This time he kept the curse behind his lips but felt it no less. Freed, he pushed to his feet, determined to take Stuart to the study where they could have a private conversation. Clearly, his man had not accompanied Sam as they'd expected. For him to have come all this way could only mean bad news. Lily didn't need to hear it in a raw form.

"I'll return soon. Kate is here to look after you."

Henry could see the moment Lily's gaze followed his to the doorway. Her thin limbs trembled, and one hand lifted toward him. She must have recognized the man's dockside appearance though she'd never met Stuart himself. "If it's about Sam, I want to hear it."

For all her frailty, there was no weakness in her tone. Lily had always been far too sharp for him to brush her concerns aside.

Shoulders slumping, Henry waved Stuart to one of the chairs. "Tell us then."

The man moved awkwardly across the room to sit. He held his hat on his knees, both hands clutching the short brim.

"I did everything you asked," he said, the words strained. "But the girl didn't come, nor you neither." The burly man had never seemed so cowed in all the times Henry had met with him.

"I checked where you usually lodge, and no one had seen you. I'd have been here sooner, but I stayed to investigate." He stumbled on the last word, strength and loyalty his qualifications rather than education.

"What did you find?" Henry could tell the man had more to say, but the delay offered no kindness as Lily's breath started to catch in her throat, signs another coughing fit threatened.

Stuart hung his head and stared at his hands for a long moment. "The news ain't good. You would've sent word if you didn't send the girl, what with paying for the tickets already and all, so I went out to find what might have become of her."

"And?"

Finally, Stuart looked up to meet his gaze. "I found no word of a girl, but there were a steam carriage crashed something horrible heading for the docks. From the luggage, I'd say a lady of means were in it, but there weren't nobody by the time I learned of it. The police took off the driver and the carriage stood empty. Asked the fellow watching it, and he said no deaths. I didn't get a chance to talk to the coachman, and from all reports, he took a bruising. Wasn't all that clear, if you know what I mean, when they wanted to learn the happenings."

Henry exchanged a tortured look with Lily before turning to Stuart, whose mangled hat would need some blocking before it could recover its former state.

"You are not to blame, Stuart. You did well bringing us this news, and for seeking what had come about." Henry forced his lips into a pained smile. "You must have rushed all the way here. A bed will be found in the servant quarters, and your horse is already comfortable in the stables, I'm sure. Kate here will take you down to the kitchen for some food."

Kate drew in a sharp breath, but said nothing when Henry leveled his gaze on her. Instead, the lady's maid jerked her chin and set off, expecting Stuart to follow.

Stuart rose, bobbed a rough bow, and half-jogged after the disappearing maid.

Henry released a slow breath, trying to take in all they'd learned, as little as it had been.

Stuart had been responsible for negotiating Henry's shipping interests for years. Not the full arrangements or trading plans, but making sure when one of Henry's interests came in, the workers were ready to unload and supplies for necessary restock were available.

The man was thorough and efficient. Henry never had a moment's doubt when asking him to accompany Sam to the Continent, nor had Stuart questioned the propriety of such arrangements as some would have. He accepted Henry would tell him everything he needed to know, nothing more and nothing less.

It had all been prepared with sealed letters and reassurances. Stuart remained ignorant as to Sam's true nature. There'd been no reason to stretch his devotion with such knowledge. Henry knew his staff here would keep silent about Sam as well, their loyalty without question even in the case of Kate.

Still, Stuart's ignorance meant he could not have known to ask the right questions, and the lack of information ate at Henry. Just where could Sam have gone? She'd never been to Dover before, had no one she could turn to beyond Stuart whom she had never met, and he'd seen the flash of fear in her eyes when Lily could not come with her.

A soft groan escaped his lips at the thought of Sam wandering the docks in a town that, while not wealthy, would have its own supply of contraptions if for no other reason than sailors bringing home curiosities from distant lands. With the purse he'd given her as well, Sam could attract the wrong attention all too easily without Stuart to guide her.

$\mathcal{T}$HE SOUND FROM HENRY BROKE through the ice surrounding Lily. She'd been trapped in the realization that all their plans had fallen apart. She had no one to blame but herself.

"How can Samantha ever be safe now?"

Lily hadn't meant to say the words aloud but was too caught up in her own fears to keep them bottled inside. She could feel the tension coiling within Henry as her head once again found his shoulder.

He kept his touch gentle, wrapping his arms around her and gathering Lily to him as if he could protect her from this truth the way he'd protected Lily and Sam both from the law all these years.

"Sam's a smart girl." Henry's voice rumbled against her ear. "She's able to manage on her own. It hasn't been so long since she kept quiet in the abandoned stables in London."

As much as she wanted to cling to his reassurance, and his warmth, Lily pushed free. "You don't understand. She was safe in the stables, and though she had little to amuse her, she kept calm. Now, she'll be tired and frightened. Maybe even injured in the crash. She won't have me to prevent a bout, and she'll know I won't be coming any time soon either. You've never seen her scared before. Any control she's managed strips away faster than you can blink. How could I have let her go alone?"

Henry caught her hands, holding them tightly even when she tried to tug them free. She had no choice but to meet his earnest gaze and let him see the tears gathering in her eyes.

He smiled, though where he found the strength, she could not fathom. "I know you're worried. I am as well. But look at the truth before us. Listen to what Stuart uncovered."

Lily shook her head, not in denial but rather because confusion swept her. "I do not know your meaning," she said, her words as faint as her strength had become with this discovery.

Henry released her then only to rise and pace about the room, his arms waving to punctuate his words. "When he made inquiries, rumors of the carriage accident had spread through the docks. He learned of it even when he hadn't been present to see the event himself."

She murmured an encouraging sound, clinging to his sense of hope when she had none of her own.

"Don't you see? If Sam had lost control then, the carriage would be the least of the news people would eagerly share. Stuart spoke with what must have been a police officer on site. The officer would have given warning if news of an out-of-control Natural had been making the rounds. Such a rumor would spread as quickly as the carriage tale if not more so, filled with exaggerated descriptions of every mechanical device she'd transformed into a metal defender."

Lily could see the truth in his statement at last, but her strain didn't ease.

Her sister was still out there among strangers, in a place she knew not at all and surrounded by those who would seek to gain from her more than to assist her, at least until they learned the truth of Sam's nature. Then they'd be all too ready to help her right into an asylum.

Henry knelt before Lily, catching her hands a second time. "She must be fine. She survived the crash, and if I know our Sam, she figured out some way to get to the Continent with or without our help. Surely she could devise a plan to make inquiries of her own as to the ship. Perhaps Stuart had left his post by the time she found the right vessel, but she's wily enough to sneak aboard on her own. Just think of the trouble she's been up to here at the estate. She's no quiet lady no matter how much you'd like to see her so."

"What if she couldn't find it? What if the ship had already sailed when she learned its berth? What if she's wandering the streets of Dover, or already been taken by some ruffian?"

Though his shake held little force, Lily's teeth cracked together when she'd thought them already clenched as tight as teeth could be. It did succeed in breaking her of a growing panic as she settled her dazed vision on his determined expression.

"Remember how delighted she was with the idea of going, Lily? She wouldn't let something simple like missing the ship stand in her way. She's been dreaming about this as far back as she can remember. Sam used to tell me of it when we first came here. I took her tapering off as a sign she'd found happiness, but it's clear she only gave up her dream for yours and mine. We were selfish in holding her with us this long."

He'd meant to reassure from how he started, but even Lily heard the bitter twist in his final sentence. She put a hand to his cheek and held it there until he turned into the caress and laid a kiss on her palm, a small thank you for her sympathy.

The right answer came to her then, and her hand dropped. "Go there yourself. Go to Dover. Find word of Sam. Stay as long as it takes."

When he began to shake his head, she caught it between both hands. "I'll be fine here on my own, and better knowing you'll learn just what happened to my little sister. I cannot stand not knowing, nor do I think you'll rest any easier. She might be as smart as you say, but Sam has never been on her own. Even if she managed the ship, would she know to send word? She could be resting safely within the haven and we'd never learn of it."

Henry looked as though he would argue, but Lily only firmed her gaze. "You know I'm right."

The breath went out of him on a deep sigh, and he pushed to his feet. "You are, as is usually true. I just don't want to leave you now when you are suffering under such strain."

Lily managed a smile that held against any wavers. "I have Kate and Cook and the whole of your household to watch over me. Neither am I such an invalid as of yet to need a nursemaid."

A cough spoiled her determined statement, but though his eyes narrowed, he gave a stiff nod.

"I'll go if for no other reason than to bring back something to ease your mind. If she's there, I will find her. If she's not, there must be some evidence of her whereabouts. I have business to conduct in Dover regardless. I'll stay as long as it takes to complete my work so none will question my presence there, then I'll return with whatever news I've been able to obtain."

He'd caught the fever of her possibility now, and Lily knew nothing would keep him from it, a knowledge supported as he strode half out of the room before turning back.

"I'll send Kate in to attend you while I prepare for the journey. I leave at first light with Stuart as my companion. Highwaymen will be less likely to take on two able-bodied men, and we'll get there faster astride than by carriage. If there is anything to be found, I will find it."

Lily watched him swallow the distance to the servant quarters with the full measure of his long legs, a pang burning in her heart. She hoped he would find word of Sam to bring her and so comfort them both. If her sister had done as he supposed, though, they couldn't expect to learn anything. The only time news would come of a stowaway would be if she'd been captured. In that instance, Lily doubted the label attached would hold any connection to how Sam snuck aboard.

She clung to the promise Henry had given in that rumors of a Natural would fly from tongue to tongue faster than any other even when no truth existed to support the claim.

Those with the talent to transform mechanical devices as if by magic might be fugitives in the eyes of the law, but fascination with their knack drew others to the vicinity as much as fear kept them wary. A single slip, and Sam would become the focus of everyone's attention, with none holding her needs at the fore.

2

Henry left with Stuart before Lily had risen the next morning. If there were any chance of finding Sam in Dover before the authorities did, Henry had to move quickly. Lily might have found his words reassuring, but two days would have passed by the time they arrived. Two days in which Sam's fear could only have grown.

He cursed the decision to let Sam go by herself, the pace offering little to distract from his thoughts.

He'd been so caught up in how weak Lily appeared the day Sam left, he'd failed to realize the comfort his wife would have gained by knowing that her sister had reached the ship and Stuart's charge as expected. Or rather, he had not considered the likelihood of disaster.

Henry had only agreed to Lily's safe haven plan because he thought giving up responsibility for Sam would strengthen Lily. Yet, she seemed weaker now. The strain of caring for her fugitive sister couldn't compare to that of not knowing what had happened to Sam.

Hope kept Lily fighting, and she had little enough to hope for now.

The pattern had been thus for longer than he dared to contemplate, visible each time he brought Lily to see a doctor. Despite the effort required to make the trip, she'd grown stronger with hope. Only once they'd returned home and the

truth of her condition—or rather, the absence of a cure—
sank in, did she weaken again.

He could not accomplish what the doctors had failed to
and offer a cure, but neither could he watch the love of his life
fade away while he did nothing. If she needed hope, he would
go find her some, and when he found Sam, he'd convince her
to stay at her sister's side. Her presence offered more strength
than it stripped away, something only revealed once Sam left.

Henry shifted in the saddle, his thighs sore even through
the thick canvas trousers he'd chosen to wear so he could fit in
with those who might have the answers he needed. It had
been some time since he'd spent this length on horseback, and
any calluses had softened long ago. They'd made a brief stop
for food and a stretch around midday, but otherwise, they'd
kept to a steady pace so as not to harm their steeds. Though
he wanted to dig his heels in and approach the port city at a
dead run, Henry doubted the stamina of the horse Stuart
rode, coming as it did from a hire stable.

Sam had been as much child as sister to Lily, more so even
when the babe who'd taken root in Lily's womb lacked the
strength to survive. If Lily ever thought she might have con-
ceived a second time, she'd kept her counsel from him just as
she'd spoken not a word of the first to her sister. Her womb
stood barren no matter how much they both longed to fill his
old manor house with the sound of running feet and laughter.

Only then she'd had Sam.

He knew it pained Lily to think the Stapleton line would
end in this generation. Though the world little resembled his
grandfather's time, Lily knew better than most the need for
those willing to work for the betterment of others. It used to
be bloodline to separate the classes, yet wealth had taken that

role as much as any claims to nobility, both elevating some and dropping others from the ranks of those with the power to act.

Henry had once thought to use his own position to change how Naturals were treated much as he'd protected the lower classes when an officer of the law.

Instead, he'd been distracted by making house and home for Lily and Sam, a distraction he'd welcomed then and would have for the rest of his life. He could not question Sam's eagerness for a place where she could be free, nor could he fault her for it. He had no right to keep her from such a haven. No right at all. But for Lily's sake, he'd beg Sam to return.

"Lord Stapleton, will you be staying at your standard quarters?"

Stuart's question startled Henry when the other man had kept silent for so long he'd almost forgotten he had company, but a quick glance at their surroundings revealed the reason. They'd come upon Dover unnoticed while he'd been lost in thought.

"Not this time," Henry said, considering his purpose in coming. "I need a place down by the docks where people might be a little more free with their stories and eager for a new ear to bend."

His man gave a quick nod. "You'd best be asking after your daughter there. The gentlemen of means would only question your capabilities as though nothing ever went wrong on their watch."

Though Henry hadn't considered that aspect, Stuart had a fine understanding of the wealthy, whether they came from a long pedigree or newly joined the ranks on the back of some grand invention. He chose to contradict the man's belief in

Henry's meaning no more than he'd revealed Sam's true connection to him. She might as well be his daughter as much as Henry cared for her, and it did not speak well for his keeping that she'd been lost.

"I know just the place. Not as rough as some, but kept busy by sailors with coin to spend. And they've a good room or two set aside for when harsh weather delays boarding. If the better establishments are full up, those of means are happy to pay for a clean bed to lay their heads."

"Sounds like just what I need." Henry might have missed the outskirts, but now he worked to keep his horse level with Stuart as the road suddenly filled with people. Most came from nearby labors, but the streets also swarmed with merchants come to hawk their wares in the evening hours just as they flooded the streets in the wee ones before the workers were off to fields or businesses down on the wharf.

The horses won free near the shipyard where sounds of heavy industry continued despite the late hour.

Henry shuddered at the thought of Sam finding herself in such a space. What had once been mostly wood now contained as many workers outfitting the grand steam engines or producing parts that engineers could use to perform repairs while out at sea. There were many strong machines to trigger Sam's nature no matter how she struggled against the demand.

He'd toured the facility once as part of his investigation into this new steam transportation when he had interests in several sailing vessels and owned one outright. As much as he would have loved to share the experience with Sam, surely any such choice would have ended in disaster. If not for the sake of Sam's freedom, he would never have considered bringing Lily's sister anywhere nearby. The cost to the shipyard, and all those dependent on it for their livelihoods or safety on the open waters, would be high if a Natural lost control within its walls.

His seat in the House of Lords might have come from his title, but he kept it not through bloodline alone. His business acumen won him the standing while others holding only hollow titles slowly lost their hereditary rights to someone of more industry. Last he'd heard, a seat no longer required even the indulgence of an honorary title, The Queen having recognized the benefits of keeping such gentlemen out of the Commons. Or perhaps she'd bowed to the pressure of wealth as other kings and queens had to the demands of nobility in earlier days.

He could not speak to the difference, having stayed away from London almost entirely in the past five years since Lily sickened. Henry knew only of his secured status by matter of messages urging him to take a stand for the old ways or strengthen the voice of those members with shared business interests, both sides determined to use him to their advantage.

His lips curved at the memory, aware—as most were not—how little his family held the old ways in awe. A title still had its benefits even with each quiet change reducing its value. But never had those of nobility proved to be without the same failings found in any class of people. The older the ways, the fewer he'd found untainted by the corruption of power. When one could determine the course of a life simply by saying the words, remembering the value of each and every one of those lives appeared more difficult for the successive generations.

The faint smile twisted into a frown as Henry longed for the days when he could serve the people on a beat and his brother would be the one to lay judgment as to their continued happiness. Though had he stayed, he could never have kept Sam at his side. He would have had to give in to Lily's request so long ago to send her and Sam off to the Continent alone, much as he'd given in to Lily this time.

He'd no more wanted to lose Lily to a safe haven then than he wanted her to succumb to illness now. This time, though, he'd found himself powerless in the face of her weakening with no options to offer, none other than that which Lily herself proposed and Sam eagerly adopted.

A choice he now had cause to regret.

"Here you go," Stuart said, swinging down from his horse before a building Henry would have dismissed as a tavern alone if not for Stuart's knowledge. "I'll bring your horse off to the stables where I hire from. They'll take good care of 'im and be ready when you are to return home. Just ask for Peg and give my name inside. They'll do as well for you."

Henry raised both eyebrows at that even as he dismounted.

"Now don't you be givin' me that look. She's my dear wife's sister that she is. Peg'll do right by you, and you can trust her not to let on to your standing, if you get my meaning. Folks round here might not be as rough as some, but could be they're not comfortable telling tales among more refined ears."

Henry clapped Stuart on the back and handed over the reins. "I get your meaning and give you my thanks. Your assistance is valuable as always. If I'm to succeed, it'll be half on your head."

He didn't think to the implication until Stuart dropped his gaze to stare fixedly at the ground.

"I am sorry I lost her," he mumbled.

Henry waved a hand low enough for the other man to see despite his tipped features. "It was no more your fault than if a storm had cast the ship onto strange shores once she'd joined you on it. You've done more than most would to help even so, and I appreciate it. Now get you home to your dear wife who's sure to be wondering what you're about."

That brought Stuart's face up once again, this time with a grin. "Don't you know it. But she'd want me to do right by your girl as I would with any of my daughters."

Henry choked down a flash of jealousy as he turned to enter the establishment. It seemed cruel that any man could have such a wealth of children, four daughters and two sons, when Henry had none, but if any deserved such a bounty, Stuart numbered among them.

HE IMPRESSION OF A TAVERN space continued when Henry pulled open the heavy oak door and stepped inside. An older sort of establishment, this tavern must have served sailors for generations past. He lacked a builder's eye, but he'd wager the horse Stuart led off that the beams, and perhaps even the wood making up the benches and tables, came from masts split in ocean storms.

"Whatcha be having?"

The man behind the worn bar bore little resemblance to the aforementioned Peg, but Henry approached anyway.

"I am just up from the country with some business to attend to. I'm seeking lodgings and meals more than a simple drink."

The man looked him up and down in a fashion Henry felt sure could catalog every aspect of his clothing and bearing to determine whether he'd be warming a seat at the table or standing beside it. Henry had dressed to ease suspicions, but suspected the man would see through the disguise of rougher clothing.

Before the barman could announce his conclusions, Henry held up a hand. "I'm to ask for Peg. Stuart sent me. Said you kept a decent establishment with rooms to let."

That brought a smile to the man's face. "Stuart brung ya? He's even more particular than that wife of mine, so you must be worth the trade. Peggy!"

The bellow set Henry rocking on his heels, but sure enough, a red-cheeked woman bundled out of the back, a mock scowl on her face.

"Now what you be bawling about, my husband? I have enough to deal with of a moment. Supper's coming faster than the sun can find its rest."

"This here is Peg," the man said with a nod. "She'll see you set up with a room and a meal right quick. He's a friend of Stuart's."

Had her husband not added the last, Henry felt certain they would have both been on the wrong end of a tongue-lashing, but his man's word held weight not just with the barman.

"That the way of it? I'll have one of the girls prepare a room. You give him a mug of the better ale. Sit you down wherever there's space and supper will be out as soon as it's ready. When you're done, just ask George here for the key and directions."

Almost before he could thank her, Peg turned and strode into the kitchen, already calling instructions.

He exchanged a laughing glance with the barman as he accepted the ale.

"She's a good woman, and I'm a mite bit lucky to have her, but she was born with a set of lungs on that one."

Contemplating Peg's robust nature only brought back the circumstances of his own wife and the urgent need to bring her some comfort. Henry turned to sweep the room with his gaze, seeking just the right company. The barman and Peg might have expected him to choose one of the small tables to the side, but he marked the length of the main table and the prospects already seated. They seemed the type to share a tale or two.

"I'll be over there when the meal is served," he said, leaving the bar without a second glance.

His supposition proved grounded as he heard the one word he'd hoped to find none of when he took his seat.

"What's that you said?"

The sailor turned to face him, eyebrows raised, but didn't complain at the interruption. Rather, he shifted further back on the bench so as to bring Henry into the tale.

"I was telling old Bill here about how some fancy bloke all in a stiff suit caused a ruckus up on the docks a few days ago. He said some poor street urchin was a Natural out to change his boy's train when she only snatched it up after it went missing. From what I've heard, she gave it over right fine when the boy saw her about it. The man, though, would have none of it. He set all the able-bodied men after her. Ways I heard it, he didn't even join them, not and scuff the shine off his shoes."

Henry stared at the sailor, his worst fears come true. "What happened then?"

The sailor laughed so hard at the sight of Henry's expression he threatened to tip backwards off the bench. "You needn't worry of a wild Natural in these parts," he gasped out at last. "That scrap of a girl disappeared into the gutters where she must have been hiding from the grasp of the workhouses, and they lost her. No contraptions rose to defend her, nor did any of the wagons become music boxes like they say can happen. Iffn you ask me, I'd guess the fancy bloke took one look at the crowds and decided to thin them out a bit. He sure dragged his boy kicking and screaming up the gangplank quick enough. That girl was no more a monster than I'm a right gent."

Laughing with the others, Henry kept his true feelings hidden this time. He'd expected to work hard before discovering what had happened to Sam, but who else could it have been? How they'd mistaken her fine dress for scraps, he didn't know, but she had a way of attracting every smudge to be found, and after the carriage crash, there were sure to be many about her.

Peg arrived then to pass around bowls of aromatic stew made with a good helping of strong ale from what he could smell. He'd been hoping for a cottage pie, but this, and the loaves of coarse bread served with it, would fill him up and offer an excuse to linger in hopes of hearing more.

The sailor might have dismissed the man's claims, but Henry knew better than most that Naturals did not have to be monsters, nor would every simple contraption call out to one. He should have been relieved, but this only proved she'd be unlikely to have slipped aboard her ship undetected. Between the sailors on alert for a Natural as they'd be even if they doubted the man's claims, and her being chased off, the chances of Sam getting back to the ship in time seemed weak at best.

That didn't mean she couldn't have found another vessel to take her. He hadn't lied when he'd told Lily Sam often proved resourceful, and with this story in the wind, people would be much more suspicious whether they sought a wild Natural or just a girl with skill enough to survive on the streets. A girl didn't last long out here without taking on some kind of a master, and they tended to know just who worked their territory.

The stew, though delicious, soured in his stomach at that thought. Sam would do poorly whether picked up for her looks or her quick fingers, those eking out a living on the streets more interested in what a good tidbit could buy them than any form of solidarity from what he'd seen in London. Those who ran the youngsters were worse. They forced the pretty and frail to do the hard labors, knowing police were more likely to go easy on them while the master grew fat on what his ratlings could pickpocket.

Henry scraped the last bite onto his spoon, unwilling to waste energy he'd be sure to need in the coming days if he were to discover the truth. Whether she'd left the port long before or even now lay cowering from a beating, he would not rest until he knew just what became of Sam. Or at least that none of the worst had.

3

Kate swung open the sitting room door and came through backward, a tray balanced on her arms.

Lily offered a faint smile in gratitude though she had little interest in even the tasty treats Cook was sure to have added to the snack.

The woman bustled about, plumping up pillows and bringing an extra blanket to stretch across Lily's lap until Lily bit down harsh words her lady's maid did not deserve.

When Lily leaned forward to pour the tea, Kate clicked her tongue and pushed her down. "You don't strain yourself, mistress. I'll pour you a measure. And look at the sandwiches I brought you. All your favorites."

Lily surveyed the display, her lips twitching with unexpected humor. Though she'd broken her fast not more than two hours earlier, enough sandwiches to feed a horde of visitors rested on the fancy china.

She glanced at Kate who stood not two feet away watching her. "You needn't hover. I told Henry I didn't need a nursemaid."

Kate shook her head. "The master should never have left you like this. He should be at your side as is proper." Her lips pressed together into a tight line, but the criticism had already escaped.

"I told him to go." Lily would have said more, but she'd heard everything the morning Sam left despite how they thought she'd fainted.

Kate had been good to her, welcoming her into Henry's household and ensuring her comfort at every turn, especially once she'd sickened. Measuring that against the hatred her lady's maid held for Lily's little sister, though, left her relationship with Kate shaky, and mentioning Sam would do nothing to improve things.

As much as Lily could understand why the lady's maid felt as she did, surely eight years with Sam should have gentled her heart and shown how the stories of Naturals were just stories. Sam was her sister, the last of her first family. How Kate could choose to serve her while hating Sam Lily could not understand, Natural or no.

"What can I get you?" Kate asked, breaking into Lily's thoughts and making her aware of the frown pinching her brows together.

Lily shook her head. "I need nothing but quiet. I'm sure you have duties to attend to. I'll be fine here on my own."

"If you're sure…"

Waving the novel she'd been pretending to read before the lady's maid entered, Lily smothered a smile at how her frown passed to the other woman. Kate didn't read and had no intention of learning, despite Lily's offer to teach her. Said she had no need for more than she could manage already. In this case, Kate would have been happy to learn Lily could not find the concentration either.

"I'll leave you then, but ring the bell should you need anything." Kate placed a servant's bell on the table well within reach and stepped to the door, finally leaving Lily to the peace she sought.

"Mistress. My pardon, but you have a caller. He won't leave until he's spoken with you or the master," another maid said from the doorway.

Kate's frown deepened into a scowl that sent the girl back three steps. "She's not to be bothered. I'll handle this."

The girl straightened. "He said the master or mistress only."

Lily watched the exchange without true interest. Rarely did anyone come to see them here without sending a letter in advance, and they'd been expecting to spend more time in Dover after accompanying Sam to her ship so had made no arrangements for visitors. Cook or Kate would be able to manage the man regardless of what he'd told the maid.

Her gaze drifted to the book in her hand but she could not remember anything of the story. She set it on the table and stared at the mantle clock Sam had so longed to touch. Lily would have given anything, certainly a clock for all it had been in Henry's family for generations, just to have Sam here with her.

Lily knew she should be grateful for this home filled with luxury and history. She no longer had to worry about where their next meal would come from, and for the past eight years, Sam's safety had not been in question. Now, it seemed she'd only delayed the inevitable.

She wished she'd convinced Henry to come to the Continent with them when they were all in London. Lily would have been happier in a hovel in France with both Henry and Sam at her side than here, surrounded with luxury and yet so alone.

The door swung wide once more, this time with enough force to smack into the wall.

Lily turned to meet Kate's glower, but before she could ask what she'd done to deserve it, a tall man stepped around the maid.

"Apologies, mistress, but he just will not go away."

Staring at the man, Lily sought the answer to why he seemed familiar and found nothing. Still, whatever scrap of memory hinted at knowing him came without fear, and the deep sorrow in the man's face drew her as nothing else could.

"It's fine, Kate. He clearly needs to speak his words. I'll ring when he's ready to leave."

Lily could see the hesitation in Kate's expression, but the woman would not ignore a clear dismissal, at least when a stranger stood within earshot.

The lady's maid left the door wide open, though whether for propriety or as a reminder others were nearby Lily couldn't say.

She waved the man to a seat. "There are plenty of sandwiches should you be hungry. You'd be doing me a favor in truth. I can ring for another cup as well." She hadn't thought of the lack until now, or she would have sent Kate for one promptly.

The man, a servant by clothing though one of higher rank as such things were measured, stood shifting from foot to foot, his leather cap held between his hands and a cloak slung over one arm.

Lily let a gentle laugh escape her. "If not for your own comfort, then for mine, please sit else I get a crick in my neck."

Only after she spoke did Lily remember the last man to take the chair she offered had been Stuart come from Dover with bad news.

That gave her the hook she needed to pry loose her memory of this man standing proud beside a shiny vehicle. "You're the coachman. Of the steam carriage."

Where she'd expected the recognition to bring him ease, instead his head hung low as he refused to meet her gaze.

"I've come to apologize." The words released in a gruff whisper. "I swear to you I've never had a crash before."

Suddenly she understood why the man seemed so distraught and scolded herself for not considering just how the accident would appear to one who did not know of Sam's nature.

"You are not to blame. Accidents do happen."

He shook his head with a vehemence that brought his gaze up to meet hers. "Not like this. We'd been delayed on the road, and I drove the carriage faster than ever before in the hopes of making up the time and making sure the little miss made her ship boarding. When we needed to slow once in Dover, she'd built up too much speed, the carriage had. Nothing I did would make her stop, not until she ran full force into a wall."

Lily gasped, a hand rising to her mouth to stop the sound too late.

His head sunk a second time. "I took a crack on the skull fierce enough to confuse me. The police came with all their questions and took me off before I could remember to check on your sister. When I returned, this was all I found."

He held out the cloak she had thought to be his own, though she should have recognized its feminine lines, and waited for her to take it.

Somehow, the cloak made everything real all at once. She hesitated, but couldn't very well leave the man with arm outthrust.

A crinkle of paper when she accepted the offering only made Lily's fear burn hotter. What else could it be but the letter Henry had written to introduce Sam? She'd been left on the streets of Dover with nothing to show as proof of her position. She could be swept up into a workhouse for all Lily knew.

The pain in the coachman's eyes brought her back to the moment. The man blamed himself for Sam's loss, a burden he should not have to bear when Lily knew just what had caused his carriage to run wild.

Lily gave the cloak a shake and forced a laugh between stiff lips. "My sister is always losing things. A less mindful person you could not imagine. She left the loss out of her short message when she found my husband's man, but you're a wonder to bring it to us. I accept your apology. You were not to blame, especially when you yourself were injured."

"I made the carriage go too fast. After all my boasting, I could not stomach missing the ship."

She shook her head even before he finished speaking. "You'd been delayed by my own self until too late, and you said there was trouble on the road as well. No matter how fast the carriage, sometimes there are obstacles that cannot be overcome. And you brought her to Dover in time in any case."

She regretted the falsehood but much better he think Sam safely delivered to her ship after all. Already some of the gray in his skin had pinked.

"Are you sure you won't have a sandwich?" Lily offered for lack of anything else to say.

He pushed to his feet, the cap crushed in one hand. "No, mistress. I best be going. Thank you for hearing me out and reassuring me. She's a fine girl your sister and I couldn't bear thinking I'd brought harm to her."

She smiled at him, hiding the pain in her own chest. "I'll ring for someone to see you out, then."

"Thank you. I'll wait in the hall."

Whereas she'd been longing for solitude before his arrival, now Lily wanted to call him back. She bit her tongue.

As much as she'd needed someone to blame before, she could not put the weight on this man's shoulders. He no more deserved it than did the carriage itself, though for the police to credit the accident to an overpowered carriage was much better than to suspect the nature of the girl who had once been inside it.

She sipped her tea only to find it gone as cold as her heart.

She'd suspected what had happened before, but now she knew with surety. Without her there to settle Sam, and after delays in leaving and on the road, her sister had given in to the engine's demands for speed. Sam wouldn't have meant any harm, but from the sound of it, she'd given speed in such a way that removed the ability to control or stop it. Her sister was not a craftsman. She did not understand the workings of the things she changed as one who built them for a living would. This was why Lily should have been there.

The cause of the accident fell squarely on her own shoulders. Sam might have done the transformation, but had Lily been there, her sister would have been able to control her knack. Nor would they have been so late in the first place.

Sam had needed her just one last time, and she'd failed so completely that her sister now wandered the streets with nothing.

Memory teased and Lily reached for the cloak the coachman had brought her to be sure. She patted down the pockets, but still found no weight or clink of coins. The small purse Henry had given Sam was not here.

Lily clung to that realization.

If the coachman had wanted to steal, the cloak itself would have fetched a better price than the purse held. While Henry's letter would have eased her way, at least Sam had enough coin so she would not starve.

4

So you'll be headed back home on the morn?"

Henry lifted his mug and took a deep sip before answering Stuart. For three long days, he'd made discrete inquiries about the Natural rumors as he conducted his business, often enough with Stuart at his side. But whether he spoke with dockworkers, captains, or the local businessmen, Henry had been able to discover nothing more than he'd already guessed.

Stuart pressed a hand to Henry's shoulder. "I'll keep my eyes open and ears listening for any sign of her. If there's ought to learn, I'll be here to capture it."

Surprised at Stuart's awareness though he shouldn't have been, Henry grimaced. That he'd been looking for information about Sam had been clear, but had the connection to a real Natural been as obvious? He couldn't know without asking, the one sure way to spread the truth of Sam's nature if it had somehow escaped Stuart.

"Thank you. You've been nothing short of a wonder since I came across you that long ago day. I do not know how I'd manage without you."

A flush tinged the other man's features red. "'Tis no more than any would do. You pay me well enough to manage your interests, and like as not, most others wouldn't see market bargaining as a sign of ability, especially not one such as you."

Henry laughed at that. "You forget just who I was then, or rather what I'd been a short while before." Memory rose of his days with the police and made his current inability all the harder to accept. His team would have helped him canvass the neighborhood, seeking out the least clue to lead them to wherever Sam had hidden or been taken. At least if she remained in England.

He missed the sense of purpose and camaraderie those years had offered.

"True enough. You had quite the reputation in those days. Word spread even as far as Dover about the nobleman officer with a mind for the little folks. There's some who mourned when you gave it all up to sequester yourself in the country with your new wife."

With a shrug, Henry tossed aside his wistful thoughts of the past and said only, "She was worth every sacrifice."

Stuart let loose a full belly laugh. "Sure and I know how that can be. I'd do anything for my lovely wife, though perhaps that's to protect my own self considering who suffers when she's out of sorts."

Henry stared into his mug, seeing not the level of rich ale but his last sight of Lily. She'd been so weak he'd have cheered to have her rail at him over the slightest thing.

Again, Stuart closed a gentle hand on his shoulder. "You'll be back to her soon enough. You've arranged the next trades for as soon as your ship reaches the harbor and worked out some possibilities for selling off what she carries even. There's nothing to keep you from your wife."

His lips twisted into the semblance of a smile as Henry gazed upon Stuart in silence. Finally, he sighed. "I've done nothing you couldn't do on your own, have I? With the exception of authorizing some funds, you no more needed me here than my horse."

"Ah, but I enjoy your company."

"Don't you listen to a thing my sweet-tongued brother-in-law says. He's happy to see you for the excuse to linger in the tavern rather than run after that horde of his. And happier still when you cover the account."

Stuart went to protest Peg's interruption, but Henry felt no need for even friendly bickering.

"I'll know my charge now, if you please, Peg. I'm heading off tomorrow so should get a good night's sleep."

"You're decided then?" Stuart seemed neither eager to be done with him nor attempting to change his mind.

Henry gave a deliberate shrug. "You've made it clear enough I'm not needed here." He softened the words with a smile. "And my lady wife is just as eager for my return as I am to be there."

Stuart sobered. "At least you should be able to tell her with some measure of confidence her sister is not locked up in a workhouse nor taken in by one of those who uses the street urchins. This here's a small community. New faces are noticed."

"If they'd have said anything to me. As you mentioned, it's small, and I'm not here often enough to be a regular."

"Not in these parts, it's true." Stuart drained the last of his ale and wiped a sleeve across his lips. "But I stood at your side through most of the asking, and put word out that you were both my employer and a friend. They would have told you if there was something to be said."

Henry pushed to his feet, stopping to clasp Stuart on the shoulder. "You're a good man, and a good friend, but you're also right. There's no more to be learned here, and no reason to leave my Lily building up fears for lack of knowledge."

"Aye. You'd best be on your way, for her sake if none other. I might not have the police experience you are known for, but I can check in with the ships returning from the Continent as well as any other. Like as not, she used your purse to buy a corner to curl up in on one of the smaller ships. What you'd consider enough for a solid meal goes a lot farther when one wanders to the lower docks."

Answering the posit with a faint smile, Henry turned to the bar to settle his accounts.

However Sam managed to quit Dover, he could not see any way she might have remained here. By now she would have been out of funds and desperate. Word would have spread like a wildfire just as rumors of Naturals in London reached every ear no matter how wealthy or poor within a day or two regardless of how much truth or falsehood lay behind them.

He started up the stairs to his room, his business done and with no recourse but to cling to small hopes as he returned home. Even had she found a way aboard a ship, there were still many dangers between here and the safe haven, especially with her not knowing the exact route. He'd do Sam no favors by starting the very rumors he'd been seeking.

He could do nothing at all for her now except pray she came through it all safely. Even should he manage to set the laws of England on their ends, no change would happen fast enough to make a difference in this case.

*T*HE TRIP HOME FROM DOVER took longer than going forth, though whether because his horse had grown fat and lazy on the stable's feed or he was in no rush to tell Lily what amounted to nothing, Henry could not tell.

Lanterns hung beside the stable doors as he came up, his home eager for his return regardless of his mixed feelings. He wondered if they'd had the lights out every night since his departure, but he couldn't scold Lily for the waste, not when the very sight brightened his mood.

The stable boy appeared then, reaching up to take the reins from him.

"Any word of Miss Samantha?"

Henry smiled at the eagerness but had to shake his head. "She's not in trouble in Dover. That's the best I could determine."

The boy nodded and headed off as soon as Henry swung down.

"I'll bring your bags in soon," he called over his shoulder before Henry could say a word, most likely wanting the chance to share his news with the household first.

Henry watched him leave, reminded again how Sam had many friends at the manor who missed her and worried after her as much as Lily and he did. What he'd said would run through the lower halls quickly, and he didn't want Lily to learn of it second hand. He stretched his legs in a loose stride, happy to walk off the stiff muscles in any case.

Again, light greeted him despite the sun having found its rest some time before, but even more so, the door flung open as he mounted the steps, a watch clearly having been kept on the stables.

"The mistress is waiting for you in the sitting room," Abigail said, the maid making an awkward curtsy with sharp elbows pointed to the sides.

"Thank you," Henry murmured, not even stopping to hang his coat and hat. Lily had been waiting long enough.

He paused at the sitting room door, stunned by Lily's appearance as she lay on the couch with her eyes closed.

Her bright yellow hair lay limp around pinched features that seemed all too pale.

Henry must have made some sound because she blinked awake right then and struggled to sit.

He rushed forward to help her, and she laughingly pushed him off.

"I can sit on my own," she told him, proving her appearance frailer than the reality. "Tell me what you discovered of Sam."

Sinking into the chair nearest Lily, Henry dropped his hat to the table so he would not mangle its brim. He let a sigh go free as he sought how best to tell her, but delaying would offer no aid.

"It's as though she vanished from the face of the earth. I asked everywhere. She might have had some trouble on the docks, though I cannot be certain it was her, despite charges of a Natural, because no one believes the man's account. And after that, nothing. Someone must have seen her, but she passed so unremarkably, or was there such a short time, she made no impression at all."

He stared at his hands, unwilling to see the despair in her face.

"That's good, then, isn't it?"

Lily's question brought his head up.

"My sister isn't the type to fade into the background with her red curls and mischievous nature even with her knack under control. If they haven't seen her, it's a sure sign she made it aboard a vessel."

Remembering the stable boy's question, Henry had to concede the truth in her thought. Sam would be hard to overlook.

A spike of fear thrust through him then. What if someone had noticed? A smuggler captain out to make a tidy sum.

Even as the thought swept him, he pushed it away. If she'd been kidnapped, her captors would soon learn any cage offered more to assist than hold her, and they'd deserve whatever they would suffer while Sam's creations would take her safely to the nearest shore, whether this one or another.

"What is it?" Lily leaned toward him as she asked, chilled fingers smoothing the frown from his brow.

As much as he didn't want to scare her more, if he did not explain, she'd find some worse answer. "I was thinking on what would happen to any who tried to kidnap Sam out to sea. She'd end up safely on her way, but I couldn't say the same for those committing such a crime."

Lily gave a sharp nod. "And they'd deserve every bit of it," she said, echoing his thoughts. "You don't really think that's what happened, do you?"

Responding to the tension in her tone, Henry moved to sit at her side and gather Lily against him. "To be honest, I don't think they'd manage to set sail before our Sam would be out among them, claiming the ship as her own. If the rumors of a Natural on the docks were Sam, her ability had already risen to the surface. What ship of nails and gears could stand against her?"

Lily bit her lip, her eyes wide. "What ship could even if the crew didn't take her against her will?"

He hugged her tighter, shaking his head at the same time. "Fear and desperation might lower her control, but she doesn't change things to harm. She never has even when harm came as a result, and I don't see why she would now. Her creations love her. Think on how the ones penned here fought to follow her for several days before they quieted. Do you really believe her talent would lead her to craft something likely to harm her very own self?"

"It's what made me think she'd made it safely away," Lily said, her voice soft. "When they no longer tried, I thought maybe they knew she'd gone out of reach."

Henry smiled down at her. "And from all accounts, you'd be right. Maybe they quieted not just because she'd gone, but also with her headed for a better place, they needn't worry. No matter how much we care for her, she'd never be safe in England where her very nature is against the law, criminal despite any actions she might take rather than because of them. We made the right decision, and Sam's smart enough to find a way."

He fell silent, pensive thoughts taking over what optimism he'd managed along with the reminder of why he could not have brought Sam back here even if he'd found her.

Again, Lily smoothed the lines from his face. "What troubles you now?"

Henry shrugged in an attempt to dismiss his worries. "It's just I wish she'd found Stuart after all. With my letter, she should have been able to. He's well known in Dover, and well liked."

Lily gasped, one hand pressed to her lips. "I forgot. The coachman. He came here to apologize for the accident, all unaware his skill could not combat the power of Sam's knack."

Henry twisted to face her though he didn't understand what this might have to do with Stuart and Sam. He respected the coachman's actions. He would have to send word to his neighbor dismissing any blame and thanking again for the borrow. He'd even pay for the damaged carriage if the man would let him. Without Sam's intervention, the steam carriage would not have crashed, and if not for the lending of it, the carriage wouldn't have been racing to Dover at all.

"I hadn't realized until now, but I know why Sam never found your man."

Lily's words broke through his thoughts and brought Henry's attention back to her. "How so?"

She quickly explained how the cloak with his letter had been left behind in the carriage, though there'd been no sign of his purse, and how she'd thought better a falsehood than let the man bear this burden.

Tension he hadn't realized he'd been suffering eased at her description. "It says more than why she didn't seek Stuart." The first true smile in what felt like an age stretched his lips. "We know now she was neither so injured in the accident nor kidnapped while unconscious."

Lily stared at him uncomprehending.

"Don't you see? Sam, our Sam, would have sprung free of the carriage with no thought to what she needed to claim from it. Had she been taken, the quality of her cloak would make her a subject of ransom and would not have been left behind when it could fetch a good penny on its own."

"I had much the same thought myself," Lily said with more animation than he'd seen in her since arriving. "That if the missing purse had found its way into the coachman's pocket, he wouldn't have returned a cloak worth much more. You're right that Sam would be the one to abandon it thoughtlessly. She made it, didn't she?"

Cook bustled in right then with a tray, but the woman stopped short on hearing the last. "Miss Samantha made it to safety? That's a refreshing bit of news indeed. We've all been worried, so we have."

Henry gazed at the woman who had commanded the kitchens as far back as he could remember and couldn't think of what to tell her, unable to decide whether truth or letting the misunderstanding hold would be better.

"Do set your burden down," Lily said when he remained silent. "We have good reason to believe she's safely on her way, though until we receive word from her, there is only hope and prayer to keep her so."

Cook frowned for only a heartbeat before she smiled once again. "Hope and prayer that she'll have. There's most of us who loved the little miss, and if God be listening, He'll have a fill of scoldings to keep Him watching out for that special girl."

"I couldn't have said it better myself," Henry added at last. "It pained us all to let her go, but Samantha needs a place where she can be herself without fear."

"Aye, that she does. Never a more deserving soul I've seen. Anyhow, here's some supper for you as I doubt you found much to eat on the road, and tea for you both. Mistress, would you like aught else?"

"I have all I need right here." Lily caught Henry's arm and smiled.

That brought a laugh from Cook, who grinned from ear to ear as she turned to leave them.

More than just Sam had won the approval and love of his staff. Henry would do well to remember that when he worried about being gone from Lily's side.

As though drawn by his thoughts, Kate appeared in the doorway, a teacup in her hands. "It's late, mistress. You should be drinking your healing tea, not some other."

He didn't miss Lily's grimace, but when she turned to face her lady's maid, no sign of it remained.

"Thank you, Kate. You're right. I should be soon to bed. I wouldn't want to miss the drink."

Kate, ever diligent, remained to watch her mistress swallow down a brew that, from Lily's expression, must have tasted worse even than it smelled.

He'd never noticed any benefit, but it made Lily happy to accept the care of her maid, and it could do no harm. The doctors in Dover surely hadn't proposed a better treatment. If drinking this tea made Lily feel as though she did something toward healing, he would be the last to question simple things like a repelling taste and stench.

ily lay in the sitting room with a shirt across her lap, but she had not made the first stitch, her mind too busy and her hands too weak.

Henry had been so sure she'd improve, so confident, that she'd half believed him to be correct. Instead, he looked more haggard with every day passing, and she felt as though pinned to a wood block and examined beneath a microscope.

Her ears strained for any hint of Henry's return despite how his worry distressed her.

She'd sent him out on the grounds in the hope fresh air would ease his tension, perhaps thinking it would do the same for her as well. Rather than relaxing, though, she'd spent the time waiting for his reappearance.

Lily sent the mending to the floor in a fit of pique she soon regretted. She had to pick it up quickly before someone found her like this and thought she'd begun to spasm or have some other symptom to add to her weakness.

The effort exhausted her. Beads of perspiration formed on her forehead and her breath grew ragged. Had she the energy, her teeth would have ground together with her annoyance loud enough to call the ever-faithful Kate to her side.

They all worried after her, Henry, Kate, and the rest of the staff. If she had to sample one more abundant serving of something Cook put together to tease her appetite, Lily felt she might just scream. Though as little breath as clung to her of late, likely no one would notice her lapse in behavior at all.

If only her sister could have fixed Lily the way Sam had repaired the steam-powered heater. Or remade her into something stronger as Sam had numerous contraptions. Her sister thought herself so clever, but Lily knew of every little device Sam had hidden throughout the house. She used to look at them, even pick them up sometimes as though she could see into their inner selves the way Sam would. The same blood ran through their veins, yet they could not have been more different.

The house felt empty not just because of Sam's absence but because her sister had gone through and removed all evidence of her life here, every device she'd touched. It didn't matter how many servants Henry kept or how their voices came in from the hall. An energy that existed only where Sam and her creations lived had vanished, fading out bit by bit as the days passed with still no word. It had been seven days since Lily collapsed on the manor steps and lost her sister forever.

Voices came from the hall right then, among them the one she'd been waiting for. Henry had returned.

The sight of him at the door brought color to her cheek. Wind had tousled his hair, the sun brushed color on his skin, and the change had at last drawn a smile to his face.

She could remember anticipating and dreading his arrival at the bakery oh so long ago, knowing her body and mind would betray her in his presence when she'd have done better to dismiss his interest. She loved him no less for the time that had passed.

"Are the fences all well tended?" she asked, wanting to share in the respite from their concerns.

Henry strode across the room, sank down at her side, and swept Lily into his arms. "The fences are tended, the sheep are losing their winter coats to the shears, and it should be a good year."

Lily tilted her head back to smile at him, soaking in the sunlight still warming his skin. "So it was a good survey?"

"Yes, it was good both to get about and to see that the world didn't stop turning just because we froze in place."

He rose suddenly, still holding her, and Lily let free a shriek, belying her thought about the volume of her scream.

"Is all well, mistress?" Kate halted her rush to take in the unlikely sight of Lily in Henry's arms.

Lily felt her cheeks heat, though whether embarrassment or excitement caused the blush, she couldn't tell.

"I've determined my wife is in need of some time spent out in the fresh air and bright sunlight," Henry said as though coming upon them thus happened every day. "Have Cook make up a basket and send Abby along with it when she's ready."

Kate stood still for a moment longer, her lips pressed tight as though to hold back sharp words. Finally, she spun on her heel and strode off.

Lily nuzzled Henry's cheek and laughed. "You'll have the whole household talking. This is hardly proper."

"If carrying you off into the sunlight brings on your laughter, I'll make it a daily occurrence. I don't know why I didn't see it before. Of course you grow no better trapped here in the sitting room or sometimes the conservatory. You have nothing to occupy yourself beyond worries."

He fell silent at that, and she knew his mind, like hers, had flown straight to the question of Sam as it often did.

"Seven days now with no word," she whispered, feeling the weight of each hour pressing down.

Henry gave her a gentle hug. "You said yourself she's never had cause to write anyone. She'd be the first to cringe if she learned her ignorance brought you pain. Better to focus on getting stronger so we can take that trip you promised her. The manor runs fine without my hand in the mix. We could go on a Grand Tour this summer and roam all of Europe as we seek her out. Like as not, she'll be happily ensconced with gears, metal parts, and others whose greatest conflict is who lays claim to which pieces."

She let his reassurances take hold when she'd have brushed them aside just one day before. Sam was all he said of her and more. Her sister's knack might prove an obstacle but it could just as easily aid her in finding safety.

Answering his statement only with a smile, Lily tapped him on the shoulder twice. "Abby will spend all day searching the manor grounds for us if we don't get started, and she'll catch trouble with Cook for the failure."

Henry bowed, bringing forth another squeak from Lily's lips as she too tilted with the motion. "As you wish, my gentle lady. Outside we go."

Laughter rose from both throats this time when Henry made as though he were a horse to bear her. His trot had none of the jolting she'd suffered the last time he'd convinced her to go on horseback. For this moment alone, it seemed as though everything would be right once again. She'd grow stronger, they'd discover Sam had found happiness at last, and perhaps she and Henry would conceive another child to brighten their lives, this one strong enough to survive the trials all the way to becoming an adult someday.

Her joy dimmed a little when she noticed Henry turning away from the workshop. It stood as an all too tangible reminder of their troubles with none of the hope they'd collected. A short time ago, they would have gone toward the structure, calling out for Sam to leave her creations and join them in the fresh air.

He strode toward an old sugar maple tree that had stood here longer even than he'd been alive. He'd told her stories of helping the servants extract the sap when he was younger, and she could see where the drip from this year's efforts had been driven.

Sunlight striped the spot now, but the harsher light of midday would be eased by thick foliage. Henry lowered her to a rug already laid out below.

Lily's eyebrows rose as she stared at her husband. "A sudden inspiration, truly?"

Henry shrugged with a grin. "Sudden, yes, but not in that moment. I'd already realized you needed to leave the pen of the manor as much as I had. And Abby will not have to roam as far as you might have thought. I gave instructions when I arrived home."

"So you sent Kate on a fool's errand. She will not be pleased." Lily tried to give him a stern look, but the guilt in his expression prompted a giggle.

"She would have come along just to tuck you in here as she does in the parlor. The idea is to escape the confines, not bring them running alongside."

Lily patted the spot by her side, loving him all the greater for how he thought of her even when busy with other responsibilities. "Come tell me what you did today while we await Abby's appearance. It will distract you from the rumbles in your stomach."

He stared at his middle as though betrayed, but it only grumbled once more.

The laugh came easier this time, and it gave Lily hope they would find their way back from the cloud that seemed to have come to a halt above their heads. Sam would not have wanted that for them.

HENRY THANKED WHICHEVER MUSE INSPIRED the idea of a picnic as he watched the lines of tension relax out of Lily's face. He told her of chasing down an escaped lamb, the plans Mr. Simmons had for the far fields, and even the calamity that had befallen his cravat when a bird flew overhead. Once he ran out of the morning's adventures, he recounted the characters he'd met in Dover. Henry chanced thoughts of Sam in favor of introducing Lily to the wonder that was Stuart's sister-in-law, the old sea captain who mourned the days when sail was good enough for all of them, and the sailors laying every indignity on those of wealth or position in their mocking tales. Little had changed in their lives despite the upheaval among the titled folks.

Their luncheon came and went as they sat there talking, this day a time out of time, a return to when they had nothing but happiness stretching before them.

"Do you remember my plans when first we came to the country? I'd thought to take on all of London in the Natural cause."

He could have cut out his tongue for the words that tripped so easily from his mouth and the tension they caused to race through Lily's thin bones. He'd been too caught up in memories to consider the pain his mention would bring.

"You have every bit the crusader blood of your ancestors, Henry. When many would rest on their holdings, you'd cast them aside if doing so could ease the suffering of the smallest street urchin."

A flush heated his cheeks even as gratitude filled him at how she did not flinch at the thought of Naturals. "Seems to me you were the one to champion the street child in the bakery, not me."

She laughed and shook her head. "I would have given that boy some rolls. You gave him purpose and a future."

"It's Parson who took Tom in, not me. He's becoming quite the police officer from last I heard. Worked his way up from scrub boy with a reputation for being reliable. His life would have been much different had you not looked on me like a monster when I only thought to save your employer some lost wares."

"I did nothing of the kind."

"Oh, yes, you did. Here I'd thought to play the hero, and you looked more terrified even than Tom."

She pressed a hand to his cheek. "You are, and have always been, my hero." Her eyes sparkled with mischief as rich as any in her little sister when she added, "Whether I willed it or not."

Henry reared back in mock horror. "How was I to know my delicate flower harbored deep secrets and a fugitive with them?"

"The only flour I bore came from the barrels in the pantry."

Though she'd answered his quip with one of her own, they both fell silent, this time the memory of Sam too strong to deny.

They talked of justice, of protecting those who fell victim to the times and the wealth of others, but there existed no greater injustice than the Natural laws. Created from whole cloth when all others came into being based on cases determined generations ago, the Natural laws condemned all Naturals without exception.

The guilty had to prove their innocence, but how could a Natural ever do so when their very being became the crime? They were treated no better than plague rats, hunted down and dispatched without a measure of compassion. Or more like weeds in a cultured garden, torn free wherever they might spring up and tossed aside to wither and die when many a country wife found remedies in those very growths.

A soft touch on his cheek drew Henry's attention to his wife. She gazed at him with such concentration he could do nothing but stare back.

"What is it?"

Lily let her hand fall away and turned her gaze to the field beside them instead of speaking.

"Tell me. I will do all I can to help."

The laugh that came from her lips held little humor as she twisted to face him once again. "You will. You always do. But in this case my solemnity comes from fighting selfishness."

"Such a word has never described you before. I cannot imagine it's found root at this late date."

Lily blew out a harsh breath. "When did I become everyone's angel? Is it the sickness that makes you forget I can be just as selfish as any? Did I not keep Sam trapped here because I wasn't willing to let her free?"

Henry pulled his wife close against him and rested his chin on the top of her head even as they both took to staring across the field. "Only you would be upset at being considered perfect, my love, but I know your faults all too well. Had you any glimmer of an idea Samantha might be unhappy here, you would have cut the very heart from your breast to bring her what she desired. You are to your sister what she is to machinery. Driven to heal and help even when all the world would be turned against you."

She sat up so sharply he had to jerk away to avoid being smashed in the chin, but when he glanced back, she'd fixed him with a steady look.

"And you're no different. I knew it meant a great sacrifice to hide out here in the country, but you did so to keep Sam safe. Don't you see? You don't have to crush your greater instincts now. You, yourself, brought back those dreams of long ago. You set them aside then because the risk of fighting for them lay on Sam as much as on you. Now there's no cause to sequester here. You can go to London and bring justice not just for Sam but for every Natural like her."

Henry let the idea wash over him, filling in cracks in his being he'd ignored so long as to have forgotten them. Had he not railed against the cruelty himself?

"Are you sure the journey to London wouldn't be too much of a strain on you?" The question stood paramount over all others, but held within it the acceptance of her challenge.

Lily shook her head. "You need not bring your burdens with you. You'll need every bit of energy to argue with those who refuse to see. I'll stay here where the staff is well versed in my care, and I have everything I need to keep me until you return."

As much as he wanted to argue, he had only to remember how the trips to Dover seemed to overcome her upon their return. It would do her no good to take the journey, and she had no need to be there if not strong enough to visit with old friends.

She held up a hand before he could say a word. "I won't let you use my weakness as an excuse either. If you cannot leave a week or so on business, your interests will fail. And if I'd suffer such for business, how much less is my suffering worth when whole lives hang in the balance."

Lily smiled then, excitement sparking in her eyes. "Just think. You could change not only my sister's future but that of every single child born with abilities beyond those shared by most. You could set the precedent for whatever next springs from the loins of humanity. You could change the world."

Though he had already conceded the victory, he laughed at her phrasing. "I fear you give me too much credit. I am but one man."

She turned once again to nestle against him, her heartbeat strong where their bodies touched despite her frailty. "One man can move mountains if only he inspires those around him to each lift a single stone."

The idea took root and spread throughout his form.

Henry would do this. He would fight for the Naturals as he'd intended long ago before letting fear for Sam's safety hold him back. No person deserved the lot consigned to all Naturals, and if his efforts meant Sam could someday be free to come home should she wish, then all the better.

6

*I*t took three days to organize his return.

He sent word to his man of business in London and the caretaker of his London house, but the most important missive he sent announced not just his intention to claim his long forgotten seat in the House of Lords, but a request to address Parliament.

With so much resting on this first effort, he planned to retire to his study in the town house and work on just what he would say to those present as soon as he arrived. Lily, he imagined, would spend her time on daily picnics. He'd asked Kate to ensure this, though part of him wished to be there instead of on his way to speak to those with no interest in his cause.

The composition of the House had changed since the age of industry. King George IV first gave honorary titles for industry, a tradition many thought new and wished The Queen had not continued, but Henry had read enough histories to show what most nobility wanted forgotten. Many titles had been earned with a heavy purse in previous reigns, a practice with deep roots. Still, he did not know whether the presence of so many recently considered common would aid or hinder his intent.

When he entered the London outskirts, though, Henry turned his steed toward the police station rather than his town house. The station had been more a home to him in his youthful years than any residence. He'd found solace there when tragedy took every other living member of his family. Until he met Lily and learned the truth about her troubles, he'd thought nothing could pull him from its humble walls.

"Haven't seen many of your type around here in recent years."

The statement pulled Henry out of his reminiscence and brought a grin to his lips as he recognized Parson's solid tones. "Do you speak to the horse or the man atop it?"

Parson stretched up a hand and half-tugged Henry into a rough dismount. "A sign you haven't been visiting much, Lord Stapleton. We keep our own stables now. Those in charge are too cheap to outfit us with mechanical conveyances capable of keeping up with the wrongdoers, especially with us exempted from fines or license fees."

"It's Henry. I have little need for titles around you lot, and I've lost the right to officer." He laughed. "Seems to me there was a time when you'd have crowed with delight to be offered horses over anything mechanical."

Parson shrugged. "Either the contraptions have grown steadier or we've become accustomed to them being about. You cannot place a boot around most parts without tripping over something fashioned by human hands. It's a pleasure to sit astride God's work."

Henry closed the distance between them and pulled his former officer into a quick embrace. "I've missed hearing you preach, Parson. Not a day goes by when my mind doesn't stray to you and the others."

A flush tinged the man's pale skin for a moment before Parson shook his head. "You wouldn't know it by your absence." His visage sobered. "Heard tell your lovely lady has been off to see the doctor in Dover a time or two. How fares she?"

It became Henry's turn to shrug. "The doctors offer little no matter how often I bring her, but I have faith she'll weather this as she has all the struggles in her life."

Parson gave Henry's shoulder a tight squeeze. "With you at her side, she's sure to. Never known a man more persistent, and I've met my share of stubborn. Come inside. We've just returned from patrol and the whole team is assembled."

As they turned together, the tug on Henry's arm reminded him of forgotten responsibilities. "Can you send Tom out to tend to my horse? While the inspector might not object to my visit, I doubt he'll be as welcoming to my steed."

Parson tutted as he shook his head. "Further sign of how long it's been and how much you've forgotten. Tom's no run-and-fetch boy any longer. He's an officer in truth, and a good one if still a junior."

Henry had realized his mistake the moment the words spilled from his mouth, but he accepted Parson's scolding as his due. "I'll just have to stable him myself then."

After stuffing two fingers from each hand into his mouth, Parson let loose with an ear-piercing whistle.

Before Henry could blink the tears from his eyes, a boy not much older than Tom had been when first they'd met sprang free of the station entrance.

"Jack, you take Lord Stapleton's horse round to the stable and see he's well taken care of, you hear?"

The boy went ramrod straight and gave a salute that would have done any soldier proud. "Will see to it, officer, sir."

Bemused, Henry handed over the reins and stood still to watch the boy until he turned the corner. "Making a habit of bringing street urchins into the station now?"

Parson clapped him on the shoulder, using the gesture to push him through the station doorway. "Tom proved such a help, we went to the inspector about paying the fee to get another boy out of the workhouse for the duty. Jack there is the third after Tom. Not all will become officers, of course, but it is one fewer to arrest for avoiding starvation, and it's some coin in empty pockets. We have enough work out there on the streets. No need to have officers doing the seeing to in the station."

Henry barely heard the last over the roar of greetings from his old team, a cacophony soon dimmed as Fitz cut through the noise to say, "What, no wrapped bundle?"

It took Henry only a heartbeat to connect the question to the fresh rolls he'd taken to bringing each morning. They'd offered an excuse to see Lily at the bakery where she worked when he first met her.

Henry aimed a cuff at Fitz's head. "In case you hadn't noticed, morning came and went a long time ago, Fitzwilliam. I thought I'd trained you to be more observant than that."

The others all took to laughing at Fitz as Henry slipped onto one of the benches, the worn wood familiar beneath his rump.

Surrounded by the team, even with Tom's surprisingly mature face looking back at him, Henry felt as though no time had passed at all. He knew these men better almost than he'd known his own brother, having faced dangers and difficulties at their sides for years. A strange feeling overtook him as he realized they'd continued to fight for those who had little or no voice while he'd hidden away in safety, ignoring a world become increasingly more complicated.

"Horses, eh?" he said, as much to distract himself as out of curiosity. "Seems I remember Jim being none so fond of the four-footed beasts."

Jim flushed a bright red at that and mumbled something Henry couldn't catch.

Fitz gave a broad wink. "Jim's found one to his liking sure enough. Slow beast who should have been put out to pasture, but the inspector keeps him on just so Jim here won't have to stay in the station when we're given a mounted patrol."

If anything, Jim's color deepened.

Out of kindness, and a little fear the officer would lose consciousness from the rush of blood, Henry asked for their latest adventures.

"I suppose there isn't much of excitement out there on an estate," Peter said. "You must miss it."

"I do at times, but there's enough to keep me busy. I've the sheep, of course, and my shipping interests."

"Word is you've earned yourself a seat in Parliament as much by your industry as your bloodline." Parson gave him a sideways look. "Thought you had little interest in politicking after so long despite what you said when you left."

Henry waved his hands in surrender. "Your communication lines run clean down to Dover so I guess I shouldn't be surprised you've heard of my requests right here, but can we pretend for a little while I am no more than another officer. Don't you still share the sweetest tales once you pass on the watch?" He had other needs to know the way of things in London, needs that had to do with his plan to address Parliament, but he intended to keep his purpose quiet until then so none could marshal support against him.

"You heard the man," Parson said, his tone commanding. "Bring out your favorite nabs, but don't be adding anything to the tale. Officer he may no longer claim, but he knows a false telling from a good one."

The comment raised another round of laughter before the men set to bringing Henry's understanding up to the current day.

He listened intently to every word. What they found mere entertainment offered Henry instruction he could obtain no-where else, not even in the old halls of learning that had long since turned to the teaching of trades alone. More than any-thing, he sought mention of Naturals. If these men held anger or bitterness toward those unlucky souls, he feared there would be little hope for a willing ear among the wealthy and old bloodlines.

$\mathcal{L}$ ILY STARED BLINDLY AT THE orchid Henry had bought for her several years before. A bud already threatened to open, the conservatory close enough to its pre-ferred climate even though summer had yet to reach them. It had been a gift to celebrate their child.

Henry wanted to throw the flower away when tragedy struck, but she hadn't let him. She'd said then at least some-thing could bloom.

"Mistress, the sun is setting. You should come away from there. Night brings a chill through all those windows."

As always, Kate's voice held more of the scold than defer-ence, something Lily found a comfort. She'd never have made the transition to fancy lady, not when good days had her beg-ging Cook for a corner to bake Henry one of her special cakes. Instead, her lady's maid had become a cross between a friend and a nanny, always urging her to get up and about, making sure she drank her tea, and telling her things would get better.

Her smile faded at the last, but when she rose, her gaze tripped over the orchid once again.

It had been taken from its home and brought here much like she had, but the flower managed to bloom each year. Strong and persistent. Words she'd heard often enough sent in her own direction.

"Come on. Let's get you out of here and into the sitting room where the fire's already roaring. Cook made one of your favorites. I can bring it in on a tray."

Lily pulled against Kate's hold on her arm. "I think I'll eat in the dining room tonight."

As soon as the words left her lips, she added, "If that won't be too much trouble."

The smile that lit Kate's features proved answer enough without the "I'll go tell the others to prepare your place as soon as I get you settled."

It had been all too easy to let the effort go, to slip into being treated as the invalid she claimed not to be. The time had come—or had long passed if she were being honest—to prove the weight behind her assertion she didn't need a nursemaid, a position hard to maintain while Kate tucked a blanket around her on the couch.

"Go on with you," Lily said. "The others will need to know soon or Cook will complain the meal has gone cold."

When Kate finally left, Lily released a sigh. She did not feel as though she had any hope of improvement, but she didn't have to dwell on that fact. However many days, weeks, or even years remained, Lily decided then and there to make the most of them.

Henry had finally set his sights on something to devote himself to, a cause important enough to help him survive when she did reach that point. The least she could do would be to keep him from worrying over her in the meantime. She could not change the truth of her state, or that no matter how many doctors Henry had taken her to, none could offer any aid. But she'd taken to giving in to her weakness, a choice that only made her weaker and proved a distraction against Henry's higher purpose.

No longer.

Lily tossed the blanket aside and rose. Just the thought of Henry's expression should he return to find her eating in the dining room and not requiring a tray gave her the strength to cross the room without Kate to lean on.

For Kate, as much as Henry, she needed to do this. It was not fair to those who cared for her. She might not be able to change the outcome, but she could very well change how she faced it.

Abigail froze when Lily entered the dining room as though the maid expected a scold. Her eyes widened at the sight of Lily, and a broad smile lit the girl's homely features. "Mistress, I am happy to see you here."

The maid glanced back at the incomplete table setting. "Though I'm not quite ready yet."

Lily waved a hand to dismiss the concern, locking her knees only just in time to prevent a fall. "No need to worry. I can sit over here while you finish up. I'll be out of the way."

Abigail colored bright red. "You are never in the way, mistress."

Lily took the statement for what was intended and offered only a smile. She feared teasing the girl would cause a faint as nervous as Abigail appeared to be.

The chair she'd chosen offered a welcome support, Lily only realizing once settled how she'd selected the one Samantha had always claimed.

"It's a very different view of the room," she murmured, staring across at the fancy dishes in the china cabinet.

"Mistress?"

Again, Lily waved off the words. "Just musing. No need to answer."

The girl went back to her work, and Lily kept further thoughts to herself as she explored her world through Sam's eyes.

Her gaze went to one of the hiding places that now stood empty, surprised to find it visible from this angle.

How often had Samantha watched her creatures when Lily thought her sister lost in daydreams? Perhaps she'd been communicating silently through gestures and head movements.

Lily shifted slightly to bring another such spot into view, this one less accessible to either eyesight or reach. If she squinted, she could see a much younger Sam up on one of the chairs at full stretch.

She'd learned of the hiding spots when coming upon Sam in this very room, her sister's attempt at an excuse for climbing the furniture transparent though she'd believed her secret safe. Lily saw no reason to disabuse her of the notion when it made her sister happy.

A scrape from the other side pulled Lily's attention to poor Abigail.

"I'm so sorry, mistress," the girl said, clearly flustered by her presence. "I didn't mean to disturb your thoughts."

Lily shook her head and smiled. "There is no harm done, and no reason to be concerned. I won't tell if you don't."

The look they shared transported Lily into her own childhood. They'd had but the one maid, a girl not much older than Lily was, and they'd conspire together to hide little mishaps, at first to keep Lily's mother from worrying and then because they enjoyed the secret, unknowingly training Lily for what was to come.

Father had found another position for Jenny when Samantha showed the first signs. Lily had cried and hated her little sister for taking away such a good friend, but she understood the reasons for it once her father put about that Samantha had caught fever and died. No one could know the truth. It carried too much risk, or so they'd always believed.

"Your supper's ready, mistress."

Lily didn't even start at the interruption, too caught up in the past.

Her father had believed anyone knowing would mean Samantha's loss, but Henry had more faith in the people he drew into his life. Every person on the estate knew the truth, and each of them had kept Sam's secret, even Kate who maintained her ignorant hatred of Naturals from her reaction to Sam's absence.

"Would you like me to help you?"

Laughing at herself, Lily pushed out of Sam's chair and crossed to her own. "No, thank you, Abby. I am just in a mood today. Woolgathering."

The maid bobbed one of her awkward curtsies, all sharp corners and gangly limbs as she grew. "If you don't mind me saying so…" Abigail paused at the door to the hall, though she didn't wait long enough for an answer. "It's a pleasure to see you up and about again."

The girl whisked through the door and vanished before Lily could respond, but her statement warmed Lily's heart. She'd found it all too easy to let her impending end overtake her, ignoring the effect on those in her life beyond her worries about Henry and Sam. So much of her life it had been only her, Father, and Sam. She sometimes forgot how much Henry had expanded her world and brought many trusted others into it.

Lily swore then and there to keep up appearances if she could not keep up her strength. However short or long she had on this earth, she would pass it without being any more of a burden on those that cared about her than she had to be.

At some point in the night, Jack brought the officers a tray laden with three teapots and a good number of cups, his chores apparently completed. The men were accustomed to this service as far as Henry could tell, the latest story from Ken continuing without pause.

Henry shared a significant look with Parson as Jack took the far end of the opposite bench and braced his chin in both hands, a rapt look on his face. The boy must have heard all these stories before, but he showed no less interest than Henry himself. This one might follow Tom's path after all.

Sometime later, when the tellings circled back to Peter, the young man, though not as young as he'd once been, let loose a cough and frowned before meeting Henry's gaze. "There's one tale you haven't heard as of yet, and I think you deserve it for all it has little humor. You were with us on that first Natural hunt those many years ago."

As though a candlesnuffer went through the room, all joviality drained from the other expressions, but Henry leaned in, this what he'd come to hear.

"Often enough rumor gives us the clues to track down criminals, but it's a dangerous tool when wielded in the wrong hands."

Peter had learned a trick or two in the telling of tales since Henry had been gone, but even without his delivery, Henry tensed to hear the words. Rumor could be enemy to friend as much as foe. Something said enough times became fact whether or not it had been true in the first telling.

"…We tracked down the young man who stood at the source of the rumors, all ready for a fight and not willing to wait for it to begin. If Parson hadn't remembered your trick with the pocket watch, we'd have knocked him out and had him off to the asylum before he had a chance to react."

Henry swallowed his questions, knowing he should not interrupt the tale.

"He wasn't a Natural at all, was he?" Jack's youthful voice cut the dramatic pause, this clearly a story he had not yet heard.

Peter reached over to tousle the boy's hair, a move Jack tried to duck then had to suffer in sullen dignity. "No, Jack, he wasn't. You have good instincts. You'll make a fine officer someday."

"What do you mean?" Henry could keep silent no longer.

"We never found the true perpetrator, but as far as we can tell, someone started the rumor on a grudge, knowing the power of fear. Laid enough clues to point to this fellow without making them so obvious that any could recall the starting point. It almost cost a man his sanity, if not his very life."

Henry wanted to object, to say the results would have been the same had the man been a Natural in truth. He held his tongue.

He could not make such a statement without revealing too much of his intentions and perhaps exposing the cause behind them. These men were not stupid.

As much as he appreciated hearing the tale for what it showed about how London still perceived those born with

Sam's knack, this story proved solemn enough to make the men aware of how much time had passed since Henry's arrival.

"My wife will be worrying as late as it's become," Ken said at last. "I'd best be getting home."

Henry made no move to keep them, saying only, "Congratulations on your nuptials, Ken. I didn't know."

Ken gave a satisfied grin. "Some two years gone now."

"And as happy as ever on the first day," three of the others chorused before Ken could finish his statement, it being one they'd obviously heard many times before.

That seemed as good an end to the visit as any. They all reached their feet at once in unspoken agreement.

"I'll walk you to the stables." Parson's announcement scattered the last to linger, and soon only the two of them remained in the empty station.

When Henry went to leave as well, Parson caught his arm to hold him back. "I'm not a stupid man," he said, his tone mild.

Henry turned to his friend, remembering his own thought along those lines. "When have I ever implied such?"

Parson brushed off the response as though it were an irritating fly. "I don't need Ken's talents to see how your body came alert when Peter spoke of the Natural, nor have I forgotten your statements the day you left. You've no more buried the questions raised by that young man than I have, and knowing you, you plan to do something about it."

Henry grimaced, wishing for the first time he'd been a weaker teacher when making his team an observant one.

"You needn't worry. If any of the others saw, they'll keep their tongues behind teeth about it. You're not the only one made uncomfortable by treating Naturals the way we must, as you might have guessed from Peter's tale. Though not a Natural, the discovery came almost by accident and made stark how Naturals had no chance. Not that I'd tell the team to give one any myself, mind you. I've no interest in consoling Ken's wife or having one of the others speak to my sister."

Many might have seen only rejection in how Parson stated he would take a Natural down without giving the chance of a fight. Henry saw behind the words to Parson's discomfort and recognition of justice gone awry.

"You're right, though you don't need me to tell you so. I have come to speak on the Natural cause. We treat them like monsters and then arrest them for becoming a reflection of that reality. It does not sit easy with me."

"Nor should it. I might not have your political influence, but me and the boys have kept an ear out for the Natural kind. Figure if they must be taken, at least they can be taken by some who dislike the necessity as much as they understand it. I've spoken with each of the team, and none were any more comfortable in taking that Natural to the asylum than you and me. Every one of them could see as how they'd fight just as hard with that as the only end to look forward to."

Henry shook his head, aware of what a sour gift that would be, but something in Parson's wording caught up to him.

"Their sense comes from that long ago crisis? Not any more recent?"

Parson nodded. "That one and one other. In eight years. Seems to me if there are a few born in each round of children, we'd see Naturals in London every day. And it's not as if another team or another station has been snatching them up either. I can't see as how every mother, every father, no matter the situation, would be handing their flesh and blood over to the asylums at first touch. My sister's babe is a friendly sort, and she dotes on him. He turns up with a longing for mechanicals, she'd do anything to keep him safe, if you get my meaning."

Henry fought a smile, knowing he understood better than Parson could imagine. "So if the parents aren't passing them over, then what?"

Turning to the door, Parson headed out before replying, his steps measured so Henry had no difficulty matching them. "When you first implied the treatment should be changed, I thought you mad. Not for wanting to—I felt much the same injustice back then—but for thinking it possible. Now, though…"

They walked in silence down the darkened street. Henry remembered well how he had to give the other man time to formulate his thoughts if he expected a reasoned answer.

"If they are in every round of births, people must be hiding them," Parson said abruptly, the words startling Henry after the quiet.

"Or so I thought. Seemed to me if that's the way of it, there's more to these Naturals than we're led to expect. Made enough of an impression when I figured it, I went to the asylum to see the one we'd just put in. A young woman, she was, who'd been willing to kill all of us to keep from being captured."

Henry heard the weight behind the last and clasp a hand around Parson's nearer forearm in support of the tough decisions the man had to make.

Parson pulled free, his arms swinging faster with each step as he sped up to escape his demons. Then he stopped dead and pivoted into Henry's path.

Henry barely managed to come to a halt before slamming into the other man.

"Thing is, when I went, the orderly tried to block me from entering at first. When he couldn't, he confessed she'd vanished. I barged in to discover more empty rooms than full, but the orderly and doctor would say not one word about it."

A frown creased Henry's forehead as he absorbed what Parson told him. "What happened to them? The asylum was full enough last time I went, and not so many of an age where they would have died off."

The other man shrugged. "Whether they were murdered or rescued, I don't know. All I can say is they are never heard from again. Based on my experiences, Naturals, at least those that end up in the asylum, well, they would not be able to stay hidden if they escaped. Not if they're what we're told and have seen with our own eyes. Neither do they deserve the short drop for something they were born to be. And here's the twisty part."

Parson paused for long enough Henry fought the need to demand the rest.

"You remember the spider-like device we chased through the streets to catch our first Natural?"

Henry nodded, the street lamp on the corner shedding light here where before there'd been little.

"I've told you about how many mechanical devices have sprung up, but what I didn't say is some felt like that one. Self-moving, I mean, but not trying to harm anyone."

"What are you saying?" Henry demanded, losing patience with Parson's ponderous speech.

Parson grimaced and turned so he could walk the final length to the stables. "I have not a lick of proof beyond my instincts, but what if they're being taken? Being used to make contraptions, I mean."

That brought a laugh to Henry's lips. "Parson, I judge you a good man for pondering the question of Naturals and the justice in holding their very nature to be a crime. I've thought the same myself many a time. But to think someone could control a Natural well enough to make an industry from it? Now it's you who seems headed for the asylum."

Parson laughed and shook his head as he swung open the door to the stables. "Like as not you're right. It's a fanciful notion I've shared with none save you. If a Natural could be controlled in that fashion, why wouldn't they just control themselves?"

Before Henry could respond, Parson sobered. "Which means it all the more likely someone with industry and an eye to coin decided better to dispatch the Naturals than to incur the expense of their keeping."

A twist in his gut made Henry drag in a sharp breath as he followed the other man's train of thought. Parson might be seeing those he'd brought in as required by law, but Henry could not wipe the image of Sam caught up in the noose from his mind. These deaths could not have been a public spectacle at Newgate prison, but he could see the logic by which life-long imprisonment and death could be considered much the same, one costing the asylum more.

They stopped outside the stall confining Henry's horse just as a stable boy came forward to greet them.

Parson said only, "If you came for the reasons I suspect, you come none too soon. No one deserves such treatment, no matter what they might do."

Henry managed a short nod even as his mind whirled through the possibilities, determined to find a better answer than the one Parson had given him if only to ease the burning in his gut.

"I'll leave you to get on about it." Without another word, the officer gave a quick salute and left Henry in the willing hands of the stable boy.

Henry pressed a coin on the boy for his help, an apology of sorts when all the boy's attempts at conversation had been met with dead silence.

Though his tongue remained still, Henry's thoughts kept spinning, and each time they returned to Parson's fanciful notion. What if there could be a way for Naturals to choose the results? After all, Sam had managed a repair or two among the mechanical creatures she designed. And who's to say some of the Naturals might not serve a useful purpose if people were less afraid of their presence.

He couldn't tell whether wishful thinking or a grounding in truth served as the basis for his hope, but an answer other than murdering those innocent of any crime beyond birth rested easier on his shoulders.

8

Henry shuffled the papers he'd brought with him to the House of Lords, notes he'd made after speaking with Parson the previous night rather than the grand speech he'd been intending to write.

The other members were just now taking their seats as the afternoon session neared. He looked around to see many familiar faces, though more from his labors than from the society parties his mother had commanded him to attend. He'd been the representative for their family whenever his parents and brother were otherwise engaged, a minor obligation after they'd let him follow his heart.

The Lord Chancellor called the session to order, an action that failed to draw the immediate attention of those gathered until he called out many more times.

There had been little of interest to discuss this session beyond mundanities, or so Henry's London man of business had suggested, likely the sole reason Henry had been given approval to address the House.

Or perhaps not. He rather thought the permission had at least something to do with curiosity.

Few among the young nobility actively engaged in business before the time of industry as he had in becoming a police officer. Most left what they considered base tasks to their employees and lived off their parents' allowance. Fewer still had taken up positions considered the responsibility of the lower classes until forced to when the law required every adult male to serve in a productive fashion.

Henry had done both, and continued to do so after his parents and brother all drowned at sea, leaving him the title with its intendant privileges and duties.

The memory brought a frown to his lips even as the Lord Chancellor finally managed to quiet the last conversations and bring the first business to the floor.

Henry found it hard to concentrate on the measure, his gut churning with more nervousness than he'd felt in a long while. What he did now had as many consequences as when he'd walked into the station, requested politely to speak to the inspector, and begged the chance to serve on the street.

The comparison offered a better purpose than to increase his discomfort. It had taken many such visits before the inspector conceded Henry might have a true interest in the position after all. He had still spent every year watching Henry for any sign of wishing to leave. He'd said as much when the time came for Henry to tender his resignation. The inspector never thought Henry would stay for so long.

Henry didn't expect to change minds and hearts toward Naturals with one pretty speech. He did hope to start the members thinking, though.

None stood separate from the Natural laws. Neither rank nor wealth would protect your loved ones should they prove different. Surely that alone would make these men willing to consider the question.

A ponderous cough brought Henry's attention to the Lord Chancellor only to find the man staring directly at him.

"Unless, perhaps, Lord Stapleton has rethought his interest in addressing us?"

Henry jerked to his feet, his papers scattering all around him much like the laughter that ran through the gathered members. "I have not, Lord Speaker."

At least his voice stayed steady as he bent to collect his notes before making his way down the steps to the floor. Once there, he glanced around the room, meeting curious gazes as he went.

"Lord Speaker, it is an appreciable honor to speak from the Dispatch Box today. I aim to use your time wisely, and I can see you are all wondering what brings me before you."

His opening received a spattering of calls about his long absence or whether he'd come to the right house what with his living the common man's life.

Henry allowed a smile as he nodded. "It is true, I have both lived as a common man and been absent from London for quite some time. I left the city's service to marry, but what I experienced then, as a member of the police, has bearing on what I have to say now."

Again, the expressions he noticed held mild curiosity and nothing more, a fact he felt would soon change.

Henry drew in a steadying breath, planted his feet as though to weather a charge, and said, "I have come to address an injustice began only recently and without precedence which sets a people criminal not by their actions but by their very nature."

The silence that followed gratified Henry.

He had their attention, though he doubted many had a clue as to the group to which he referred. Most would never have considered such a thing, believing Naturals inhuman and therefore lacking personhood.

He let the quiet grow until at last he heard signs of discontent, shuffling of feet, a few coughs, and the crinkle of paper.

"I speak, as some of you might have guessed, of the Natural laws."

That brought everyone to full attention, confusion the main reaction, but some faces reddened and still other members shot glares in Henry's direction.

This time he did not wait for the noise to settle. Instead, he jumped right into the arguments he'd prepared.

"What if your bitch cast a litter of puppies, good hunting stock, and one was stolen? If that pup grew to be vicious and untrusting beneath the hand of a master who beat him, would you say the pup's nature or his treatment the cause? If the dog then bit your hand, who would be responsible?"

Some confusion remained, but more narrowed gazes met his as he skimmed over the crowd.

"You would say to me a hunting dog is a simple creature who does little harm or can be avoided much more handily, but would you not attempt to prevent the theft in the first place?"

He sucked in a quick breath, not wanting to give them time to think up counter arguments before he'd reached his point. "This is the way we treat all those Naturals among us regardless of whose get. The moment they show signs, they are torn from their families and thrust into what no one present could consider anything less than a living hell. If you were to investigate the asylums and hear for yourself the cries of those within, you would think no crime worthy of such punishment. Dante would have found his Inferno right here in London."

A voice from the seats called, "They're monsters, not people. Not even hunting dogs."

Henry pointed in the direction of the voice though he could not tell whom it belonged to. "And were they monsters when they were born? When they were nurtured alongside your brothers and sisters, sons and daughters? How is it a knack transforms them from nobility to inhumanity when that would have been in their nature from moment of birth?"

"Have you given up a child?" came another call.

He did not need to struggle to find his sorrow at the question. "No. I have no child of my own blood as of yet. I do, however, have hopes for one in the future. Who is to know whether it will be my child, or yours, who next shows the talent?" He pointed to a random member, only to have the man shrink back.

"Neither did my brother show such abilities. In my time as an officer, however, I brought a Natural to the asylum myself. My team and I risked injury and even death to capture this man, but when we saw his terror, it was a purely human emotion we all understood. I do not need to have suffered personally to understand what grief the enforcement of Natural laws can bring. I have lost enough of my family to unexpected causes. Nor do I need a Natural child of my own to see how wrong these laws are. Who are we to judge?"

That question brought forth a few chuckles, and Henry had to concede the point with a shrug. Parliament, and the House of Lords in specific, had often enough been the final appeal for cases pushed up from the courts.

He pulled the conversation back, his throat growing parched as much by the dry reception as the length of time he'd been speaking.

"I challenge you to visit the asylums. See for yourself the state this law reduces our children and our siblings to. None are free from this law, not even The Queen."

That sent a ripple through the gathering at the thought of a royal child penned so, but he could see them dismissing the chances even as the idea occurred. Anyone was at risk, but these men preferred to believe their children protected somehow.

"If you could only see their faces, see the terror as they're locked inside a place designed to torture them in the name of our protection."

"That's why we have police," a nearby man said, "so we don't have to. We can't all have spent our youth protecting the streets as you have."

Henry searched his memory to identify the man, hearing the slight in the statement. He gave a gentle smile as recognition dawned. "Not all of us were forced into honest labor, your grace. Yet I see you still hold a position here so must have found true purpose at last."

A disgruntled look crossed the duke's face but he said nothing more. His implication that Henry belonged in the House of Commons instead of here held little weight with how the world had changed.

If his greatest risk came in the form of slights, Henry would consider himself lucky. At least he'd been able to offer an honest answer to the question of whether he hid a Natural child. Sam no longer stayed at his residence, and she'd never been of his bloodline however much he'd felt her one of his family.

His chest burned, though, when he considered that his one child, had it survived the womb, would be old enough to show signs if it had been a Natural like Sam.

Henry pivoted to face the section where the newer, and generally wealthy, members sat. "Mr. Burrows, did I not hear the good news that your wife is expecting as I came in?"

The man flushed with pleasure and sat a bit straighter. "You did indeed. My first."

"And one you are sure to hope is a son and heir."

The man's brows lowered in confusion, but he responded with, "Of course."

Henry nodded, the answer no surprise. "And will you be just as pleased to hand him over to an asylum should, in a few years, he start to show interest in all things mechanical?"

The man surged to his feet with a roar as though Henry had cursed his bloodline rather than positing an all too real possibility. The members on either side had to hold Mr. Burrows in the seats while the Lord Chancellor slammed his fists down on the Dispatch Box with little effect.

Backing up with his hands raised in surrender, Henry used the same tone that could stop an escaping thief in his tracks. "This is why the laws must change. It could happen to any of us. I, for one, am not willing to cast aside my child should I have one when there might be another answer."

The babble rose until he couldn't tell if any had heard him, but at last they responded to the Lord Chancellor's demand for quiet.

The Lord Chancellor focused a glare on Henry. "That will be enough, Lord Stapleton. You have ensured none will nod off as the evening grows long, and we have issues of taxation and trade to address."

Though the Lord Chancellor clearly expected an argument, Henry felt he had sown the seeds of doubt. To press further would only ensure his dismissal.

He returned to his seat through a brace of glares. Henry wondered how many of those gathered would look around their dinner tables tonight or peek into the nursery and see the possibility of emptiness were they'd enjoyed offspring.

Perhaps one or two would take it upon themselves to visit the asylums. Even if the numbers had diminished as Parson reported, those that remained were sure to have an impact.

Henry could only hope for the right impression.

*L*ILY SMILED AT THE SOUND of children squabbling outside the conservatory window. She glanced at the trousers she patched and knew another pair would likely be added to the pile before the sun set.

"It's good to see you up and active again," Kate said from another chair where she too worked on the household sewing. "You must be on the mend at last. I told you the warmer weather was all you needed."

It was true the sun shone brighter all day and the house seemed warmer. Lily said nothing, all too aware of how often she had to sip her tea to keep a cough from taking hold. She could feel the itch even now in the back of her throat.

At least she had sweet herbals to consume during the day as opposed to the bitter tea right before bed. Kate had sweetened them further still with some honey she'd traded the beekeeper for.

Lily reached for her cup right then only to find the last sip a small one and having gone cold.

"Could you pour me some tea, Kate?"

"Of course." A frown marred the maid's features as she lifted the teapot. "It seems you've emptied the pot, mistress. I'll go right now and have Cook brew you up something tasty."

Smothering a laugh at how quickly Kate dropped what she'd been working on to fetch the tea, Lily let her own repair fall to her lap as she stared blindly out the window.

Pretending had become easier over the past few days, and Lily had to admit she felt better for it as well, but still the effort left her drained by the end of the day. At least it kept her from worrying about Sam.

No sooner had the thought crossed her mind, but her worries for her sister returned in force. There had still been no word. Surely if her sister had made it to the safe haven, someone there would have suggested Sam write even if her sister didn't realize the need. Yet they'd received nothing.

Just last year, despite reaching the age when young ladies should work on their comportment or train for a position, Sam would have been out there with the other children, playing knights with the extra fence posts and certainly not taking the role of the princess in the tower either.

Lily had only to close her eyes, and she could hear Sam's voice among them. Her sister had been as much a child as any despite her unusual talents, and perhaps more of one than most of her age.

The reminiscence brought a measure of comfort for once.

Sam had never been the retiring type. If someone attempted to take her, she'd fight with all she had in her, and if anything metal lay nearby, it would become part of Sam's army faster than her assailants could catch a breath.

A chuckle escaped Lily even as she felt renewed confidence in Henry's reassurances. If anything had befallen Sam, they would have heard rumors of the great battle it would surely have been.

All of a sudden, Lily felt Sam's presence all around her.

Her sister might be gone, but the life she'd led left many lingering memories. She'd had an impact on every single person who lived on the estate. How could its walls feel empty when Sam's energy had tucked itself into every nook and cranny much like her sister had tucked mechanicals wherever a hiding spot could be found?

A noise broke through Lily's thoughts.

At first she glanced toward the door, thinking Kate had returned with the tea, but no, the sound came from near the back wall, beneath the tall windows that gave the conservatory its purpose.

It came again, a faint scritching noise like the sound of a metal rod drawn across a slate, sharp and harsh to the ear.

Lily stood, ignoring the trousers that fell to the floor as she searched the room for a better direction.

What else but an overlooked mechanical could have made such a sound? No wonder she felt Sam's energy in the air.

As though charged by the same force, Lily crossed the room and dropped to her knees to push pots to one side or another. If she couldn't have her sister, at least she could treasure what Sam had left behind.

The noise stilled.

The mechanical must have noticed her.

Lily moved one last pot to the side and found a pair of bright green eyes.

Before she could do more than draw in a gasp, the tiny creature had spun and threatened to dive back out through the hole it had dug in the conservatory wall.

She grabbed without thinking, her fingers closing around a squirming furry body.

The kitten hissed and slashed, but Lily had it trapped as she brought the little creature up to where she could see it.

"Hello, there, little one. Here I thought you a creature of metal and magic, but you're just a fur ball."

The kitten stilled at the sound of her voice and opened its eyes to stare at her.

"I think you need a more dignified name than furball, don't you? I think I'll call you Sunshine with your orange coat."

"Mistress? Where have you gone to?"

The kitten squeaked and started to struggle once again, but Lily pressed Sunshine to her and rose.

"I'm over here. You'd never guess what I found."

Kate approached loudly, each footstep making the kitten tense more.

"Hush, Kate. Move softly. You're scaring the little dear."

If anything, the lady's maid seemed to move faster. "Just what have you there?"

Lily held the squirming body up for Kate to see. "Isn't she just a darling? I've decided to call her Sunshine."

Kate reared away from the outstretched kitten. "That filthy beast has no business being inside the house, mistress. I'll get one of the men in to take it back to the barn." She glanced down at the mess Lily had made moving all the pots and gasped. "Look at the damage the creature has done to the wall. Little monster it is. We'll have rats and who knows what coming into the house with a hole like that."

Pulling Sunshine close once again, Lily frowned at her maid. "I'm not casting her out. Sunshine has come to be my friend."

"You hardly know the wild beast. I haven't been gone so long, and I think one of us would have noticed the draft if the mortar gave way during the winter." She shook her head. "Cats have a job to do like the rest of us, only theirs is outside. They do not belong in the household."

The kitten nuzzled against Lily's neck, denying any claim to be wild as she started to purr.

"I'm not giving her up," Lily said with all the authority she could muster. Her eyes narrowed as she glared at Kate.

Though the kitten had not been one of Sam's mechanicals after all, somehow it seemed like a tie to her missing sister, and Lily would not be dissuaded.

Kate's lips pressed tight together as she stared back, her gaze drifting to the kitten several times.

Finally, the maid let go of her breath in a huff. "Well, then. You'll have to explain it to the master. I won't be having it said I encouraged such behavior, and don't expect any of the others to be happy about the filthy little beast either."

Lily gave a sharp nod, accepting the responsibility.

Just then, Sunshine reached up and licked her chin, provoking a chuckle.

Lily chose to ignore her maid altogether and walked out of the conservatory toward the kitchen.

"We'll get Cook's help in washing you up," she told the kitten, "because Kate's not far wrong about the filthy what with digging through the walls. And I'd guess there might be a scrap of meat for you to chew on as well. Maybe we can dig up an old ribbon to tie around your neck so the workers know you're a barn cat no longer."

If pretending for the people in her life gave Lily some measure of strength, caring for this scrap of fur seemed to have doubled the effect. She might have a sister to dote on no longer, but Sunshine needed her help, especially if the others responded much like Kate had.

The kitten did not have the power to wipe Sam from her mind, but Sunshine offered a welcome distraction as the days since Sam's loss stretched to two weeks.

9

enry stayed in London for a full five days, ostensibly
to follow up on his business interests as he had not
been in town for some time. In reality, his man of business
kept him well informed and had no difficulty managing what
needed to be done. Henry inspired loyalty in those in his service and a wish to do their best due, in no small part, to how
he rewarded the effort.

The true reason he delayed had more to do with hoped for
reactions to his speech, and those he received in plenty.

Several gentlemen left their cards at his residence but did
not arrange a meeting time. Looking over the fancy designs,
Henry wondered if some were meant more as a threat than
welcome.

Still others sent letters varying from condemnation of his
decision to champion violent, dangerous Naturals to quiet
statements of support, most of which ended with regrets.
They were not willing to be vocal on the topic at this time.

The first type made Henry sigh in frustration, his message
having been heard but not listened to. Dangerous Naturals
had shown themselves to be criminal in intent. They should be
treated as any criminal would. He had only asked that the taint
not be applied to every Natural any more than every man of
means should be considered a scoundrel if one of their number was found to be so. There had been enough cases resolved

through influence rather than justice when he served as a police officer to show at least some among the titled and wealthy fit that description.

The second type both offered hope and dashed it down.

He lingered over those, wondering if they spoke thus because they had to make the same decision he'd come to eight years before. How many in the House of Lords itself kept a child or sibling sequestered on a country estate so as not to draw notice?

Ultimately, though, he soon found the need to stay in London had passed. His efforts to secure another time to address the House and clarify the difference between criminal by action and criminal by birth had been met with hesitation and mention of the upcoming recess, though not outright refusals. Similarly, when he attempted to respond to the cards left him, his inquiries were met with the statement that the gentlemen were not presently at home. He'd left his cards in return, but had little hope of a further discussion.

With nothing more to hold him here, Henry set off for home, eager to see his wife and tell her what had happened. Surely Lily hadn't expected him to stay in London until he'd succeeded or been drummed out of Parliament. The manor was not so far as to make a summons impossible either. If an urgent message came, he could always take the train in, though he preferred the open road.

The carriage wheels stuttered over a rock in the road, making him laugh at his inclination toward control over comfort. Still should he have need, he could turn the carriage about in a heartbeat. Not so the great metal monsters belching smoke across the sky.

Henry left off re-reading the letters in favor of staring out the window as he started to recognize familiar landmarks, his thoughts returning to what drew him to London. As much as he'd wanted to tell Lily he'd overturned the unjust laws and could now scour the whole of England and the Continent to bring Sam safely home, she had to know these things took time. The letters showed there were some willing to listen, nothing more. Yet he had to start somewhere, and at least the whole assembly didn't stand against him.

The horses had barely pulled to a stop when he flung open the door, the letters crushed in one hand.

"Go round to the stable. My staff will see you're well fed and have a warm place to rest for the night." Henry called up to the coachman as he leapt from the vehicle. "They'll see to my baggage and my horse."

He'd chosen to hire a coach and ride home in relative comfort so he could reread the letters and decide his next approach, but any pondering had escaped his mind in favor of anticipation at the thought of seeing Lily.

Suddenly, the quiet gratitude behind those words of secret support seemed so much more than he'd first seen.

He had proof they weren't alone in this journey. Where one stood shaky against the crowd, a brace of bodies could hold off even a determined mob.

He'd left early enough that morning to arrive in daylight so no lanterns cheerily lit his path, but the sun had started its downward descent long ago. Henry didn't wait for someone to come to the door but shoved it open himself, calling, "I've come home," so as not to worry any of the staff about his intrusion.

He strode for the conservatory but at the last moment turned to the sitting room, sure Kate would have tucked his Lily beneath blankets rather than leaving her in the conservatory as the room grew chilled with the oncoming night.

But when he stood in the doorway, the couch was empty.

"Henry!"

Lily's cry came from a chair half hidden by the doorframe, but more than anything, he stood stunned with how she leapt up and rushed to meet him.

"You have her letters. Show them to me."

Henry stared at his wife in confusion, the messages in his hand forgotten at the sight of her up and about. A moment too late, he thrust the offending papers behind his back.

"It's not what you think."

The joy drained from her expression, taking with it the light in her eyes.

He caught her arm with his free hand as she turned away. "I have heard nothing from Sam, but that is still a good sign. I've heard nothing about her either. For all we know, she could have found a place to hide on the Continent as she seeks word of the safe haven. Writing us would only draw attention when she doesn't know whom to trust. She'd never do anything to endanger you. Naturals might not be hunted by the law in most of those countries, but they are still feared and hated by the ignorant."

Henry wished the last unsaid the moment it came from his lips.

Where Lily might have found comfort in the idea of Sam safely hidden, she didn't need to think about fearful villagers hunting her younger sister. Even worse, he now wondered if Sam had written and her letters were intercepted. Such missives could become ammunition against him now that he'd taken up the Natural cause, and Lily would suffer as much as he would if Sam's nature came to light.

Pulling the hand with the letters forward again, he shook the papers to distract both of them from such morbid thoughts. "These might not be from Sam, but the letters are important all the same, at least some of them."

She took a deep breath and blinked twice.

"Are you well?" He put an arm around her shoulders, wondering just what it had taken for her to surge to her feet.

Lily stepped into his embrace then tipped her head to reveal a smile. "I am well enough. Or at least better than I have been. I was just disappointed."

He brushed the hair off her forehead with one finger, the letters curled into his wrist. "I am so sorry. I wanted to show you what I'd achieved and never thought how you might mistake it."

She shook her head, the blond strands falling down once again. "You shouldn't have to step gently around me. I do worry about Sam. I do wish we'd heard from her, but I don't want you having to rethink everything when I should just be delighted to see you home."

Henry pulled her close, resting his chin on top of her head as he held her. "It doesn't matter. I'm here now."

A chuckle rumbled against him, and she pulled free.

"I have so much to tell you. I've made a new friend."

Henry smiled back, his heart full at the sight of her happy once again. Her cheeks were still too pale and her skin too tight. She hadn't suddenly recovered from her illness nor had her worry for Sam vanished, but something had restored her joy.

She returned to the chair, and he felt a flash of guilt at having kept her on her feet. But she didn't sink into it. Instead, she bent and lifted a basket.

"Isn't it a bit late for a picnic?"

"You won't find anything to eat in here. If there had been, Sunshine would have swallowed it whole."

"Sunshine?" The way she used the word made him sure she didn't mean what emanated from the great orb in the sky.

Lily lifted the edge of the woven lid, but before she could raise it fully, two white paws poked their way out.

Henry lifted an eyebrow. "Sunshine, I presume?"

A white muzzle nudged the lid further and an orange kitty leapt free only to squeal as it found the floor much further than anticipated.

Henry swept his hand down and caught the squirming bundle before it could hit the hard surface below. He raised the kitty up until their eyes matched. "A barn cat?"

"Hardly a cat. Barely a kitten."

He laughed. "A barn kitten then. Certainly not what one would expect in a picnic basket. It didn't seem to like the change any better."

Lily swept her little friend from his grasp and tucked the kitten under her chin where it nuzzled against her neck. "She is a pet. As to the basket, I keep a hand on the top when carrying it so she can't leap out. When it's set down, she's fully capable of going in and out on her own."

Henry shook his head at the sight of them, knowing this a battle he'd lost before he even knew they'd engaged. "If that kitten is going to be a pet, I presume you have the necessities worked out?"

"Of course. Abigail helped me get her situated."

"Then I have only one small objection."

Lily's glare could have melted ice, but he stood his ground.

"Out with it," she said. The only reason her hands weren't braced on her hips had orange fur with white tips.

"I think if Sunshine is to be a member of our household, you must call him by the right term."

Her eyes widened, and she pulled the cat away from her to stare at it. "A boy? Are you sure?"

Henry shrugged. "Unlike you, I grew up in the country and have spent my share of time in the barn. I'd guess none of the servants felt it their place to correct you."

"Well, hello, then. Aren't you glad I didn't call you Eleanor?"

Henry reached out a hand to scratch the cat about its ears. "That would have been a little awkward to explain to the other kittens."

"That it would have."

"Mistress, Cook's ready with your supper. And for you as well, master," Abigail said, her head peering around the door frame.

Henry stepped to one side so the maid could bring a tray in, but she only turned and left.

"What are you waiting for?" Lily asked him, the kitten secure once more in the basket with her hand on the lid. "We need to get to the dining room before the food gets cold."

He waved her through first, watching Lily make her way down the hall for a moment before striding after her.

More had changed while he'd been in London than just the new houseguest. Perhaps Lily only needed time to recover after all.

He hadn't even told her about the responses he'd received to his address. She would understand the reluctant support all the better having lived that reality her whole life, but she couldn't fail to catch the greater meaning. Though he might be the first to speak, there were many ready to benefit from casting down the Natural laws.

*L*ILY MADE EVERY EFFORT TO hide how spending so long on her feet had affected her, but by the time she had Sunshine placed on Sam's chair with a bowl of food and she sank into her own seat, her hands were shaking. She tucked them into her lap and out of sight, grateful Sunshine offered a distraction as Henry took in the placement.

"He eats at the table with you as well?"

Lily shrugged. "It seemed less lonely with company while you were gone."

He laughed as the kitten tore into a scrap of meat Cook had set aside for Sunshine. "At least I can be assured of having better table manners."

"And better conversation as well." Lily stared down the table at her husband, drinking in the sight of him.

"Which reminds me." Henry tapped the letters he'd laid by his place. "I have much to tell you about my trip."

Lily hardly noticed as Cook orchestrated the meal, too caught up in the story Henry told. He had a way about him that made the least description entrancing, or perhaps she'd just missed him all too much.

"And this is why I think there is hope to be found. It might take time. Big changes often do. But someday, Sam will be able to come home again."

A gasp came from the doorway before Lily could respond, and she turned along with Henry to see Kate standing there with a scowl on her face.

"Do you have something to tell us?" Henry's tone could not have been less inviting.

Lily hoped this would be some message from Cook about their dessert or a simple household task that brought Kate to them. The way her gut burned despite the lovely meal suggested otherwise.

She'd worked so hard to keep the topic of Sam from coming up when Kate had been present, wanting to pretend she hadn't heard everything the maid said the day her sister left. Lily wasn't sure how she would react to the full of Kate's animosity toward her sister.

"No, master. Nothing really. It's just…why on earth would she want to come back here? She's with her own kind now. It's where she belongs. Look at how she hasn't even bothered to send word of her arrival. She's forgotten all about this place and the people in it."

The words cut Lily to the bone, and an anger she hadn't known she possessed rose with enough force to push her to her feet. "My sister will send word as soon as she is able. She'd never leave me to worry, nor would she expect me to dismiss her from my mind as you suppose she did from hers. You've never liked Sam. You shouldn't say such cruel things. It measures against you, not her."

The energy drained from her as quickly as it had come, leaving her weaker than she'd felt in days. Lily didn't know how she would manage to look at Kate now without seeing such a hateful person who would malign Sam when her sister was most likely in danger, or at the very least, fearing for her safety.

"Just go," she said into the silence following her rage. "I don't want to see your face right now. I won't have such talk around me. Not now. Not ever."

"Oh, mistress, I'm sorry. It just took me by surprise is all. I didn't mean to make you upset. Hush, now. It can't be good to get all worked up like this."

Henry pushed back from the table with enough force to scrape his chair legs on the hard floor at the edge of the carpet. "You heard my wife. She does not want to see you." He closed the length of the table in a few quick strides and caught Kate by the arm.

Though the maid struggled against his grip, he marched her out past the door, leaving Lily to stare at the polished surface of the table as Kate's words tried to catch hold.

"Sam would never treat me thus," she whispered with only Sunshine to hear. "If she has not sent word, it can only mean she is unable to."

10

I t took all of Henry's concentration to keep his grip on Kate from bruising the maid. Her ill-thought-out comment had brought him back to the moment when this very same woman rejected Sam so thoroughly that she would not ride in the same carriage even to ease Lily's worries. Had Kate not refused, at least they would know what truly happened that day.

A wry smile tugged at his lips with the foolish thought.

Had Kate been there, either she would have been injured in the crash or the steam carriage might not have made it to Dover at all. While Lily calmed Sam's bouts, he had the all too strong suspicion Kate might have delivered the opposite pressure.

He scowled down at the lady's maid, realizing she'd just proved to be the same irritant for Lily, whom she purported to love.

"You will leave my house this very moment."

Kate opened her mouth but he shook his head, adding, "Don't think to argue, or I'll consider whether you'll ever be able to come back."

Tears welled up in the woman's eyes, the magnitude of her offense most likely having finally come clear.

"It's good you recognize what you've done, but it changes nothing. Be gone to your father's cottage a full two weeks. In that time, I want you to reflect on all the ways you will make up to Lily for what you said just then. How you will win your way back into her good graces now that you've sorely injured my lady wife."

He gave the lady's maid a hard shake, his anger returning. "Did you really think it would be easier for Lily to believe her sister had forgotten her? She suffered enough sending Sam out into the world. To believe her sister cared so little…"

The words choked on his tongue as Kate stared up at him with fear in her eyes.

Henry dropped her arm, knowing from how she rubbed the spot where he'd held her that he'd failed in his attempt to soften the grip.

"Go on with you. Be grateful your punishment isn't more severe."

She gave him a quick curtsy, keeping her gaze locked with his the whole time and her lips pressed together. Whether she sought to hold back more words that would have condemned her or recognized the serious nature of her offense, he couldn't tell.

"I'll be off as you wish," Kate said at last, "as soon as I make the mistress's special tea. It's all that keeps her safe. I trust you'll see to it she drinks a cup each night without fail. Your word on it."

Henry frowned at her. "You're in no position to be making demands, Kate." He held up a hand to stop further protest. "But I see no harm in it when nothing else seems to help any better. If Cook can make it up for her in your absence, I'll see she has it."

Finally taking the smarter route, Kate said nothing in response, only turned and rushed to the kitchen to prepare the vile brew Lily choked down every night. While he doubted the herbal concoction held any value, it had been a part of Lily's life for too many years, and with all the changes thrust on her in these few weeks, something familiar, even if hated, could be a comfort when everything else had scattered on the wind.

He returned to the dining room, unsure of what he'd find, but Lily said nothing as she nibbled on her meal. If she chose to ignore what had just passed when she could not have failed to overhear them, he'd give her that kindness.

Abigail entered then, her hands trembling where they held the dessert tray as though she felt the distress Lily would not admit to.

"Ah, what did Cook prepare on this night?"

The maid shot him a grateful smile as she lowered the tray to the sideboard. "It's her special pudding, my lord. The one you like so much. She wanted to welcome you home proper for all you weren't exactly expected."

Henry laughed at the censure in her tone, though he knew enough to hear the echo of Cook rather than her own annoyance. He should have sent word ahead after all.

The sound seemed to strengthen the young girl, and her hands proved steady as she placed a serving before Lily and then Henry.

He caught her arm in a much more gentle touch than he'd used on Kate. "Your mistress will require your assistance in her chambers for this week and the next, Abby."

Something shifted in the girl's eyes, a spark that made him wonder if her distress came not from Lily but from whatever nastiness Kate had done once she'd been out of earshot. He pushed aside the unworthy thought as Abigail bobbed one of her awkward curtsies, so different from Kate's measured one.

"I'd be happy to help the mistress. To serve you, my lady," Abigail said, turning to Lily for the last.

Whatever he'd thought he'd seen, the delight with which she welcomed her elevation in the household, temporary as it might be, brought a smile to Lily answered by his own lips.

"Go on then. I'm sure there's much you need to prepare." In all honesty, he had no idea what preparations might be necessary, but wanted only to have Lily to himself once again. He didn't know how long his wife's mood would stay so bright and planned to enjoy as much of it as he could before thoughts of Sam wiped out even this moment.

*L*ILY RETIRED TO THEIR ROOM once they'd finished dinner, but Henry went to his study. He planned to ponder the meaning behind each of his letters and whether any benefit could be gained from the silent support of those too fearful to come forward. As he'd suspected, his lady wife had no harsh words for those choosing to adopt a quiet stance rather than take a stand. She'd held to that position longer even than he'd known her. Only now, with no one put at risk, did she encourage him to go forth and speak.

Thought of Lily reminded him of his half promise to Kate.

He pushed back from the desk and strode through the house, not trusting to Abigail's inexperience that she'd recall the command. Nor could he be sure she'd follow it if she did considering the odd look he'd caught on her features when Kate's name arose.

When Henry stepped into their chambers, though, he came to a stunned halt at the sight of such chaos.

Lily sat at her dressing table with her hair half lowered. The nightdress that should have been stretched out across the bed lay crumpled on one corner. The warming pan, the one part of this process Abigail knew well, sat on the floor next to the bed, its heat rising and dissipating into the air rather than seeping into the chilled bedsheets.

Abigail dropped Lily's overdress onto a chair, risking who knew how many wrinkles, and turned to go to Lily's side only to stop with a startled, "Oh," when she saw him in the doorway.

From the look of this, she'd not only forgotten the tea, but half a dozen aspects of her new role along with any she'd already known.

The maid bobbed a quick curtsy, not meeting his gaze, and scurried over to Lily, clearly overwhelmed by the magnitude of her task.

Henry felt a splash of guilt as he realized he'd come to heap yet another responsibility into her flustered hands.

If only Kate had kept her tongue securely in her mouth, none of this would have been required. Then to make him promise what could only be foolishness when the reason such a promise was necessary fell squarely on her shoulders seemed unconscionable. None of the doctors in Dover could help. Why should some farm remedy make the least bit of difference?

The lady's maid had become nothing but a burden to all of them.

"Henry, do leave off your scowling. I have no wish for you to scare off my new helper."

He laughed, unaware until Lily spoke that his sour thoughts had become visible on his face. "I am sorry, Abby. I did not intend to make your life more difficult. My frown came from other thoughts not concerning you."

Turning to face Lily, Henry took in his wife, seeing for the first time how she was a pool of calm in the hurricane Abigail created.

She looked not the least bit upset by the changes he'd feared would weaken her. A smile graced her lovely lips, and a glint of good humor danced in her eyes even as her gaze swept the room to see it as he had.

"All this will be set to rights before you're ready to make your rest," she said with a wave of her hand. "Won't it, Abby?"

The adoring look the maid sent her mistress made up for every bit of inexperience or clumsiness the awkward girl demonstrated. He confirmed again his decision to dismiss the tea for this night at least rather than trouble the girl.

Forgotten, no matter how well padded its tea cozy, the tea Kate had made would have gone cold. If the brew had a vile flavor freshly made, how much worse would it grow having sat? It was clear enough Lily suffered no ill effects from its absence this one night and would suffer more, if only from the taste on her tongue, should he press the issue.

A touch on his hand startled Henry from his thoughts, Lily having risen to approach him.

"My love, as much as I miss you when you're gone, thoughts of London and the work you can do there are heavy on your brow. You should return as soon as you've had some rest."

Henry pulled her to him and laid a gentle kiss on her lips, one hand stroking the still tangled hair streaming down her back.

When he lifted his head, she gave him an impish smile that made him want to sweep her up into his arms at that very moment.

Lily tipped her head and gestured behind her with her chin.

Henry followed the movement only to find Abigail who stood to one side of the dresser, her features reddened and eyes lowered, but a smile on her lips.

He turned Lily by the shoulders and gently nudged her toward the dressing table where Abigail could finish tending her hair. "Nothing is more important than the time I spend at your side," he said as she took her seat once again. "What waits me in London can do just that—wait."

Lily twisted to see him and grimaced as the brush pulled hard on a tangled strand. Still she did not swivel forward once more. "No, Henry, it cannot wait. Don't you understand? What you do now might help us search for Sam, but it's so much more than that. Only think of those letters you received. How many suffer as we did whether in the highest branches of society or the lowest? How many fear discovery at the cost of their very lives but have little choice when they will not give up a loved one to the treachery of law?"

The calm of moments before had been replaced with a fierce determination reminding Henry of when he first discovered her secret. The time when she saw him as a man of the law, not the gentleman who'd been courting her. While he wanted to protest her characterization of something he'd upheld, in the case of Naturals, he could not. She spoke only the truth.

Abigail stepped aside when he strode up to the dressing table, making it easy for him to place his hands on Lily's shoulders and give her a reassuring squeeze. "I promise I will do everything necessary to put an end to the laws that would have stolen Sam from you. I swear I will. I ask only for a few days rest at your side when none will agree to meet with me as of yet anyway. Perhaps upon my return, the Lord Chancellor will offer up another opportunity to speak before the assembled houses of Parliament."

He laughed and shook his head. "If only I could arrange for you to speak to them. With such passion from your beautiful self, all the Lords and the Commons would bow to whatever you say, a good cause or bad. You would have been a force to be reckoned with had you come to stand at The Queen's side."

"And can you imagine me hiding Sam under my skirts while paying court to royalty? It would be a farce even before my sister grew taller than my own slight frame. No, my place is here. Yours is in London just as it was when you served on the police force. With honest and thinking men like yourself, at least the laws are laid down in a fashion to aid rather than punish."

He raised one of her hands to his lips, turning it over to press a kiss against the soft skin of her palm. "It took meeting you to open my eyes."

She laughed at that. "You flatter, but without purpose. I knew well the exploits of one Officer Henry long before you strolled into the bakery to buy sweet treats for your fellow officers. I but opened your eyes to one piece of injustice you had no way of realizing was unjust as every experience you'd had, and even the tales among your fellows, told the opposite."

He shrugged, unable to argue the point and content only to stand there holding her hand.

Lily pulled her fingers free and nudged him toward the door. "Now go back to your labors and let poor Abby see to my needs as you had commanded. If you refuse to return to London, at least send missives to those whose favor you need to curry so when you do return it will be that much more productive."

Henry met Abigail's gaze over his love's head and had to concede he'd done exactly what he'd said he wouldn't in disrupting the maid's every attempt to prepare Lily for bed.

"I'll take myself out of your way then." He once again noticed the bed warmer where it lay still, no more heat rising from the coals within. At the last moment, Henry bent to sweep it up. "And I'll find someone to heat this for you as well."

He couldn't help the dark blush staining Abigail's cheeks, but he would not have Lily nestle between chilled sheets, not when she'd seemed so much better since his return.

An odd sound came from under the bed just then. He offered Sunshine a quick salute, recognizing where at least some of Lily's energy found its source. She'd ever been one to focus on the care of others rather than herself. Perhaps in removing Sam, they'd also removed some of her will to fight that which consumed her. If so, he had much reason to be grateful for the scrap of fur, though a cat—or kitten as Lily would remind—in the bedchamber seemed all too strange an occurrence.

11

S he'd been the first to encourage Henry to get about his
tasks once more, but Lily still enjoyed the three days he
carved out to spend with her. They filled up the idle hours
with picnics under the trees and tea before the sitting room
fire. Henry read to her in his deep voice and both of them
laughed at the scamp little Sunshine had turned out to be.

Her lips curved in sleep, remembering how she'd said, "I
should have known he was a boy from the start. No self-
respecting girl would behave so."

When he'd seen the sorrow her comment provoked, Henry
offered only, "You might have despaired at making a lady from
that scrap you call your sister, but all her rough edges can only
serve to aid her now. You needn't worry that she'd hesitate
over the least thing—no matter how dirty or impish—if it
brought her closer to her objective, no more than Sunshine
here let the conservatory wall keep him locked out."

She rolled in the bed, her hand seeking Henry's comfort
even now, but only chilly bedsheets met her touch.

Lily pulled back, curling tight against the truth that Henry
had at last returned to London two days before to carry on his
crusade against those who weighed material goods higher than
the innocent lives they destroyed. He had more important
tasks to be about than just comforting her. Ones that could
very well serve to help Sam along with countless others.

Sleep would not return.

Once she started to think about her little sister, it seemed her mind ran in endless circles that would not stop to allow her any rest. She clucked her tongue to call Sunshine to her, but the kitten had vanished beneath the bed hours ago. Lily did not know how he spent his night, especially when he slept most of the day, but it would seem he could offer no more comfort than Henry in this hour.

No light leaked around the curtains, a clear sign the sun had yet to make an appearance. The house sounded hollow, empty of its usual bustle once the staff awoke, usually some time before Lily would rise.

Drawing her feet up under her, Lily scooted against the headboard and rested there, trying not to think about Sam. She wanted to focus on Henry, on the hope his efforts offered not just for her, but for Sam and every Natural in England.

She knew Henry saw her rally as a sign she would recover fully, but Lily had hoped too many times and had those hopes dashed. Summer brought some level of ease and made her feel strong enough even that sometimes she had poured the vile medicine her lady's maid called tea into her chamber pot when Kate was not looking.

Thoughts of Kate distracted her for a moment. Her maid would soon return, and Lily had missed her company despite everything. Abigail tried her best, and was a delight and a cheer. Still, she lacked the maturity to sit and chat while they worked on the mending, and had other household responsibilities besides.

Lily even half missed the vile tea Kate gave her to keep the coughing at bay. Abigail forgot the first night, and Lily had been careful not to bring it up, but the weakness stayed within her. Soon, she'd regret having gone so long without treatment.

When the winter took hold if not before, she'd be fading again as she had every year. Which brought her right back to her love and his suffering on her account.

How much better for Henry to find something to hold his interest, to distract him from what would come. If he could bring Samantha home, at least he wouldn't be left alone. No matter how much he protested, Henry needed the family Lily had been unable to provide.

His had ever been a confident life with generations stretched behind him, all working toward the same aims. For such to end here and now because of her did not bear thinking.

Her thoughts turned again to Sam and the family she represented. Henry's actions made her feel as though her sister were here already, not lost somewhere between home and a place where Sam could find refuge from laws that should never have come to be. Perhaps Sam could help Henry heal enough to seek a second wife after Lily died, one more able to bring the delight of children into this quiet manor.

Lily tipped her head toward the window, Sam's presence so strong it seemed as though she could hear her sister out by the workshop even now.

The sound that must have awoken her came again.

Before she could consciously recognize the noises rose not from her imagination but from without, Lily had already found her feet. She raced through the house, her naked soles slapping against wood and muffled on rug as she ran just as she'd told Sam not to so many times.

The door offered little obstruction. She jerked it wide, then her bare feet hit dirt.

Lily cried out and hopped a few times, her soles lacking the calluses she'd scolded Sam for, but she would not let that stop her. She didn't care if she left a blood trail any hunter could follow. She could heal later.

She limped and cursed her way around the house and over to the workshop Henry had made for Sam. The mechanicals her sister had locked up upon discovering the plans to take her to a safe haven had fallen silent after only a few days with Sam gone.

Now they bumped and bashed against the locked door, eager to be reunited with their creator. Those sounds could have only one meaning.

Sam had come home at last.

ily searched the area for the flash of Sam's bright hair as she finished her approach to the workshop. She'd forgotten the darkness in her urgency, impatient for the time it took her eyes to adjust to the moonlight enough to see without straining.

She did not catch any sight of her sister, though, and the pain in her feet slowed Lily's pace to a halting limp.

Of course, Sam wouldn't be there. If she had been, she'd have opened the doors and let her mechanicals free at last.

The thought did little to depress.

If they reacted at all, Sam must be near. Lily had only to wait for her sister, and their fears would vanish.

A shadow lay against the workshop door when Lily thought the moon's rays would illuminate the whole. With the sun starting its creep above the horizon, though, the moon's strength had weakened.

Still, curiosity drew her closer, needing to know what cast the shadow. The moment she could make out what lay there, a hand came to her lips to stifle a gasp.

The mechanicals rattled the door ever louder, but Lily could not take her gaze off the dark-haired child crouched against the workshop door as though it offered some form of salvation. Little hands lay pressed against the rough wood as if trying to find a way inside.

Lily realized the girl could not reach the lock Sam had put into place. She moved closer, waiting for the child to notice her, but Lily's presence sparked no reaction.

She put a gentle hand on the girl's shoulder, and the girl shrieked a sound so sharp Lily jerked away to press fingers against her ears.

The girl collapsed to the ground, her whole body shaking and her teeth chattering though the air held only a slight chill.

Lily dropped to the dirt as well, putting both hands on top of her folded knees, well within sight. She made no attempt to reach out or touch the girl again, only sat there in silence for a long while.

When her feet started to ache, pressed as they were to the rough soil, Lily gave up on waiting for the girl to speak first.

"Where is your family?" Lily asked in a soft voice. She wondered if the girl came from one of the Romany caravans and had wandered off in the night only to end up here. With her dark hair, she could have been a wanderer, which would explain the fear. Few welcomed more than the occasional tinker, and then only if he left as quickly as he came.

She received no answer to her query beyond the girl sitting upright, so Lily tried again with, "What is your name, child?" At least then she'd be able to ask about.

The little girl shook her head so vigorously she almost knocked herself over, proving she understood the question well enough, but something kept her tongue between her lips.

"I can't very well help you if you don't give me something." As much as she tried to keep her tone gentle, Lily could hear the edge of frustration in her statement and expected the girl to recoil in fear.

Instead, the child raised her head for the first time, revealing brilliant blue eyes in a pale visage for only a second before she twisted to stare at the workshop doors.

"You don't want to be in there. It's not a good place to hide for all it might look one."

The distance from the house and anything else must have drawn her to the workshop where the stables were already occupied by stable boys. That the girl sought refuge could be assumed from both her actions and the refusal to reveal who she was.

"Did they hurt you?"

She hadn't meant to speak the question, but Lily knew all too well that not every parent or master was kind or gentle. She could only hope whoever found Sam would be a good soul.

Again the girl shook her head, but her gaze never strayed from the workshop doors.

"Well, then, they're probably worried sick about you." Lily pushed to her feet and held out a hand. "Let's take you up to the house and get you clean. We can find your family in the morning."

Though she didn't shriek a second time, neither did the girl allow for the touch, pulling away and pressing hard against the doors.

Lily put both hands on her hips and shook her head. "I already told you there's no space in that workshop for you to stay, and the house is much more welcoming. I don't bite." She added the last with a smile, her mind on Sunshine's constant nibbling.

The girl spared only a quick glance in her direction before turning back to the workshop doors. "Can you let me in?" she asked in a quiet voice. "They need me."

It came Lily's turn to stagger a step or two as she stared at the scrap before her. "What did you say?"

"The doors. Can you open them?"

Though she'd asked the girl to repeat her words, the second time lacked the very phrase Lily had rejected for all it still resonated in her ears.

She knew full well what had come from those lips, words she'd heard before from Sam more times than she could remember, mostly when her sister had been of an age to this girl or younger and her father had set a mechanical object out of reach. Sam would ask polite as ever if Lily could bring it down, as though it had ended up there by accident.

The memory brought tears to her eyes from missing Sam and her father both, but she gave this girl the same answer. "No. I cannot."

Sam had locked everything here for a reason, and that reason stood now more than ever with Henry taking on the Natural laws.

Another sharp memory rose then, of the little acrobatic man Sam had adopted when they lived in London. Her sister had said it missed the Natural who had brought it to life.

For just a moment, Lily wanted to press her own hands to the workshop, to share her grief with the mechanicals Sam had created, but opening the door would only bring harm.

"Not now," she said, softening the refusal despite everything. "First let's see about getting you warm and fed. Would you like that?"

Whether Sam's creations knew better than to make demands on a stranger, or the thick wood separating them muffled the mechanicals' cries, this girl showed no sign of falling into a bout. For the first time since Lily found her, the girl looked straight at Lily.

"I am hungry," she said in the same overly polite tone she'd used from the start.

If not from a noble family, this girl had still been raised to manners. Lily wondered how she came to be wandering only to realize the answer stood on the other side of the workshop doors. The mechanicals had never reacted to Lily's proximity no matter how often she came here to think on Sam's whereabouts.

It mattered not. Lily would never stand here and let a little girl starve, laws or no laws. Nor could she let one so much like her little sister suffer when she had the means to assist.

As though the offer of food went some distance to earning a measure of trust, the girl slid one hand over Lily's and closed small fingers around it.

Lily recognized the acceptance in this move and gave a small laugh. "We'll have to be quiet as mice. We wouldn't want anyone to catch sight of you like this."

The girl gave a quick nod and turned toward the manor house as though she'd determined its location before.

Lily started back the way she'd come, trying her best to mask the pain of injured feet.

The girl's clothes might be dirty and torn, but unlike Lily, she wore shoes with thick leather soles, a further sign she came from an established family. A better example of how cruel the Natural laws were Lily could not imagine.

This child had been neither abused nor left to want. Her presence here, her unwillingness to reveal her name or her family, pointed only to one thing.

She'd been discovered, and rather than let her be confined in one of those hideous asylums, her family had told her to run. They'd loosed a child who couldn't be much more than five years of age to wander the countryside alone as a better fate than what the law would demand.

This, more than anything, more even than Sam's uncertain state, proved the workshop doors must stay closed. Henry must be given whatever he needed to make a difference so he could change such unjust laws. He must be protected from anything that would stand in his way.

13

enry had not returned to Cooper's Bakery often in the years since marrying Lily, but he'd woken before the sun with a craving to revisit his old London haunts.

In the past two days, he'd accomplished little except to arrive and renew his requests to address Parliament. He'd be just as happy to speak to both houses, or the Commons alone, if it would get them thinking about his cause. Henry knew, however, the heaviest resistance lay in the House of Lords where those with enough coin to own the mechanical devices at risk held sway.

He'd yet to receive approval of any sort.

The time away from home, especially when Lily had been doing so much better, bit as hard as the frustration of being denied a chance to speak. In some ways, an outright denial would be less annoying than the delays those in charge of the schedule set before him.

The jangle of the bell over the bakery door caught his attention. The sound once announced an opportunity to spend another moment in Lily's presence, but now it meant only the shop had opened to customers.

He knew Bettina would be there, but whether Jane and Kate had found themselves rich husbands so they labored here no more he could not guess. It would not be for lack of trying, that much he did know. Henry had not bothered to ask Lily for the latest news, though he knew she corresponded with Bettina. There would have been no point as he hadn't planned on stopping by.

Henry crossed the street, his mind drifting to another young woman named Kate.

Perhaps he should go home just to be there when the lady's maid returned from her father's to make sure nothing else went wrong.

His frown smoothed away and he laughed aloud at the thought. Lily would be able to handle Kate as well as she'd always done, especially with her strength renewed by a scrap of fur.

"Now isn't that a welcome face to see. In you come, Officer Henry. Don't stand at the door and let the cold through."

Bettina's familiar voice brushed aside any worries about the lady's maid as he stepped the rest of the way through the door and let it close behind him. The street hadn't been all that cold, but the principle stood.

"It's just Henry now. I am no longer a member of the police force, as well you know."

She shook her gray head. "I can't very well call you that even though you took our very own Lily from right beneath our noses. It's officer or my lord for the likes of me."

Henry gave Lily's friend a broad grin. "It'll have to be officer then for all I don't deserve the title. I was never a lord in these environs, and being a lord doesn't mean what it once did in any case." It had never held much weight for him.

Jane appeared from the back and dropped a quick curtsy in greeting. "You forget we ferreted out the truth for all Lily tried to shush us. You might not have been acting the lord, but lord you were."

"Jane!"

Bettina's tone had changed not one whit since Jane had been a troublesome young girl eight years earlier.

A laugh her only response, Jane set about getting the bakery ready as the early morning custom would soon grow thick from his experience.

Bettina caught his arm and drew him over to the other counter. "So I can fill the trays while you tell me how Lily fares."

Henry shrugged, unsure what to tell her and even less sure of what she already knew.

"Lily tells me you've taken up your seat in Parliament after all this time," Bettina offered as though guessing his confusion. "I hope that means Lily will soon be joining you here in London."

He glanced down at the trays only to realize she loaded the fancy jam pastries the station loved so much.

"Could you pack up a dozen or more of those pastries for me?"

Bettina gave him a close look, as though fully aware of his attempt to stall, but smiled. "Your usual order, then? Sounds like Officer Henry is the right title for today at least. The boys down at the station will be delighted, I'm sure."

Henry shook his head, amazed she'd remembered the order, then he recalled the likely reaction and groaned. "Delighted is not quite the word for it." But he refused to change the choice when he knew under all their teasing they would, in truth, be just as Bettina had said.

"She's not planning to come, is she?" the older woman murmured with her attention ostensibly on wrapping up his order.

He didn't know what to say. Even hinting at Lily's illness made it seem all too real when he longed to believe her current state would only improve. And maybe it would. Why worry her friends needlessly?

"Lily has her own concerns on the estate so has not mentioned the possibility to me, but I'm sure if it comes about that I'll be here most of the time, she will be back. Of course, her new companion might cause a bit of a ruckus in town." He stopped there, knowing he'd have to wait only a short time, and they'd provide all the distraction he needed.

An unfamiliar woman came from the private area then, not as young as Jane and Kate had been, but clearly younger than the two women already present. He drew her into the conversation with a look.

"My Lily has always been a bit different from the general folk as some of you know. Now she's taken up with a barn cat—or rather kitten—that clawed and chewed its way through the wall of my home."

"No. Really?" Jane laughed. "That puts over anything I've done."

Bettina only finished the packaging and waited for the payment as she said, "That's our Lily. Always taking in strays no matter what they might be. Sure you remember the street boy."

He handed over his coins and lifted the package with a wave. "I sure do. I'm off to see him right now. He's become an officer, in case you didn't know."

From the grins on their faces, they knew all too well what had become of Tom. It seemed the others had kept up this tradition of his even without Lily to draw them.

*B*Y THE TIME LILY BROUGHT the girl to the house, the quiet of before had been replaced with morning activities. The murmur of voices and clatter of pans just barely reached them through a door thrown wide to let in the morning air.

Lily paused to wipe her feet on the dew-encrusted grass near the door, but still she feared her bloody footprints would give them away.

They were almost to the staircase when the solid thud and crunching roll of a log dropped onto the fire grate reached them from the dining room. Lily pulled the girl into the sitting room only a heartbeat before Abigail strode forth, busy about her morning task of setting the fires.

Lily went to step deeper into the room, but the girl held her fast, pointing to the carpet. It took but a moment to realize why.

If she placed a foot on the weave, her print would stain.

She bent down to whisper, "Across the room by the embroidered chair. My sewing basket will have socks waiting on darning."

The girl gave a quick nod and scampered across the room, returning not with one but two pairs of thick winter socks.

They shared a conspiratorial glance that reminded Lily of Sam back when their father had still been alive. The girl helped Lily layer the socks over her bloody feet so they could make their way without leaving evidence.

Cloth made for a slippery foot covering on the well-polished wood, but with the banister on one side and the girl on the other, Lily safely achieved the upstairs in time to hear one of the maids exclaim at the discovery of her bloody marks.

"Would you look at this? And all the way into the sitting room even. I suppose we should count our blessings that creature didn't pull whatever it caught across the carpet. Abigail!"

Lily no longer had to wonder at Sunshine's nocturnal activities. It seemed the kitten had not left his barn cat profession behind as well as Lily supposed.

She felt a flash of guilt at the kitten taking the blame, but better he make the sacrifice than for it to come to light just how she'd obtained this girl child.

"Here we are at last," Lily said, stepping into her chamber. "And with none the wiser."

Steam rising from her dressing table brought Lily up short, but Abigail must have taken pains not to wake her in the delivery and so had missed the fact that no one lay among the tossed covers.

Though the water would normally have cooled more by the time she rose, today its heat would serve them well.

"Come over here, and we'll see if we can't make you a little more presentable."

The girl came willingly enough, but she must have spent many days if not weeks surviving like a wild child. The dirt encrusting her proved rather difficult to remove.

The girl squirmed and fought against the hard scrubbing Lily found necessary, but the girl's strength didn't last, further showing how long she'd been on her own. By the time Lily declared herself satisfied, they were both exhausted.

Lily wrapped the girl up in the spare blanket from the end of her bed and stepped away. "Well don't you look the prettiest little angel under all that dirt. I'm sure I have one or two of Sam's old dresses that would fit you well."

The girl glanced toward her discarded clothing, but Lily shook her head.

"After all that work to get you clean, putting on those would make it undone. I can have the dress washed, though it will require more repairs than will keep it nice. Better a rag bag for that one."

"Why does Sam have a dress?"

Lily had been talking as much to fill the silence as for any other reason, so the low-voiced question startled her.

"Why wouldn't she?"

The girl stared. "Because Sam is a boy's name."

Lily laughed, having become so accustomed to the name she never considered how it would appear to others. She started, realizing how thought of her sister had brought joy rather than pain, and not just this once since discovering the girl.

"My little sister's name is Samantha. She just preferred Sam."

"Oh."

"What do you like to be called?"

"Bell. It's a girl's name."

Lily shook her head then smiled at the little girl as she pulled on a robe and crossed to a chest, which held some of Sam's old things that Lily had hoped her own children would wear someday.

"Then Bell it is. You can stay with me if you'd like. Only I think maybe we should keep how you came here to ourselves. You'll be an orphan come to live with us. Would you like that?"

Bell's eyes opened wide, and she stared around the room before giving a quick nod.

The girl looked about to say something when her mouth opened even wider and a distinctive rumble from under the bed made Lily laugh.

"Well, then, I'll just have to introduce you to the family. Though I'd guess from the noise you've met the first of them."

In the time it took to find something close to Bell's size, the girl had collapsed into a puddle of bedding on the floor, a furry bundle established at her side.

"He's a rapscallion as you might have heard, Bell, but he has a way of winning us over." Lily suspected Bell would prove the same, though from her behavior so far, rapscallion was not in her nature.

The girl stroked a hand down Sunshine's back, and he stretched into the touch, drawing a giggle from her lips.

"And he's a bit of a distraction. We need to get you presentable before Abigail comes to open the curtains. Leave off, Sunshine, and let the girl get dressed."

"Sunshine," Bell murmured as she dutifully rose with only a quick glance at the kitten.

Lily held up the dress to pull over Bell's head. "If you think it a girl's name, you'd be right. I mistook him for a female kitten at first, though how I could have, I do not know."

Bell giggled again, ducking her head when Lily tried to catch her gaze.

"You might as well tell me," Lily urged, happy to see Bell relaxing a little more.

The girl disappeared into the fabric for a moment before two thin arms wriggled free and tugged the dress down to reveal eyes sparkling with suppressed mirth.

Lily pushed away the instinct to tickle the answer from Bell as she might have Sam, knowing the girl still withheld her full trust.

Bell sobered as she stared at Lily, and a frown wrinkled her brow, but she didn't look away. "It's only your sister wears a boy's name and your boy cat a girl's," she said at last, a hint of apology in her tone.

Lily laughed again, startled by the astute observation. She looked for Sunshine only to find her pet cunningly dragging what looked like a hairpin beneath the bed.

"You are quite an intelligent child, Bell. It could very well be Sam's boyish behavior that led me to see a girl in my rude little scamp." She bent to sweep the offending kitten up, ignoring his squeal as she plucked the hairpin free and rested her chin on his squirming head.

"Is Sam like me?"

Lily froze at the question, her inattention enough for Sunshine to wriggle free and fall into an undignified heap on the discarded blanket.

Recovering herself, Lily twisted Bell so she could do up the buttons along the back. This dress survived Sam so much better than the rest because it required assistance to put on. Too often, Sam would have chosen something she could secure from the front or before tugging it into place.

"What makes you think so?" Lily asked well after the silence had stretched too long.

Bell shrugged. "You understood what I meant, and you didn't run for help."

Lily turned the girl a second time and knelt in front of her, catching Bell's hands in her own. "As I said before, you are very quick, but just because I didn't run doesn't mean everyone is so agreeable. It would be best if we never spoke of it, and if we pretend you're not. Do you understand?"

Though Lily never used the words, Bell clearly knew what she meant. Though her fingers twisted in the cloth of her skirt, the little girl gave a nod. "I can pretend. I have done so before."

Lily pushed to her feet, giving an affectionate rub to the top of Bell's head. "Somehow I thought you might have. Now how about a ribbon for your hair then I'll take you down to meet the staff. Cook will be delighted with a mouth to feed, especially a hungry one."

"I can be that." Bell jerked her head forward twice in eager nods. Then she stilled. "How many are there?"

Drawing Bell over to the dressing table, Lily kept her voice casual. "There are many on the manor itself, as many needed to keep a property of this size profitable. In the house, there's six if you count the coal boy, seven once Kate returns. You don't need to meet them all at once if it scares you, but I'll stay with you the whole time."

As she finished speaking, Lily secured the ribbon in a bow, the simple style appropriate in one so young. "You look absolutely lovely and have nothing to worry about. Every one of them will fall all over themselves to make you happy. They're a good bunch."

Bell wrapped her fingers around one of Lily's hands, her grip a little tighter than comfortable but not enough to scold the girl.

"If they're half as nice as you are, I'm sure I'll like them, too."

The simple statement sent Lily back eight years to when Henry first brought Lily and Sam to his country estate. The resilience of the young—or maybe it came of being a Natural—still amazed her.

"Come on then. Let's get some of that meal I promised you."

If her voice wavered at the thought of what this girl, and Sam, had suffered, Bell made no comment as they quit the bedroom in search of food.

14

enry's arrival at the station was greeted with smiles all around, even from those officers not on Parson's team. Or perhaps they saw the paper-wrapped bundle in his hands and knew they'd get a share of whatever didn't get eaten.

He returned the welcome with nods and smiles, wondering both at how many faces remained familiar and the presence of a good number he did not recognize. Like as not, they came in from another station. He'd have heard if crime grew so great the city had to increase its force in large numbers.

"I see you let Fitzwilliam's disappointment the other night push you to act," Parson said as Henry lowered his bundle to their table. "I would have thought you made of sterner stuff."

Henry puzzled over the comment before he remembered how Fitz had teased him when he'd stopped in the first time. He glanced around for the officer, but Fitzwilliam did not appear to have arrived as of yet.

"It's more that I wanted to relive my officer days," he said to distract Parson. "And I thought you would appreciate the gesture."

One of the others snagged the wrapped package and drew it across to where Peter and Jim began turning back the folds. Ken realized what it contained before the rest and started laughing.

"It's not the work he's missing but rather our ribbing. He's brought us the fancy pastries."

Henry shook his head. "I seem to remember the lot of you enjoying them more even than the ability to tease me."

"What's this about teasing?" came a familiar voice from behind him.

Henry twisted to greet Fitzwilliam only to have his friend grow oddly quiet. The officer thrust a hand behind his back as though to hide something.

"Is there a problem, Fitz?" Henry asked with a deceptively calm voice. To meet his friend's gaze, he had to rise from the bench, leaving him perfectly placed to take a quick sidestep so as to see what Fitz hid.

A startled laugh burst from his lips at the sight of paper wrapping to match that already on the table.

A flush colored Fitzwilliam's cheeks though he shrugged and brought it forth with apparent nonchalance. "My offering isn't half as sweet as yours."

"But equally welcome," Tom said, his voice much higher than the other men for all he tried to lower it.

Fitz handed the bundle to the youngest of the team who peeled off the covering to reveal steaming hot rolls.

"I guess we grew accustomed, and it's not as though I have another to spend my wages on."

Henry narrowed his eyes. Something about the flippant account didn't quite ring true.

"You're courting one of them," he stated baldly, the deepening red on the other man's face removing any lingering doubts. "And after you were so quick to warn me away."

Fitz snagged a jam pastry and took a large bite in what Henry would have suspected a delaying tactic if not for how the other man's eyes closed as he savored the mix of tart and sweet.

Parson put a hand on Henry's shoulder. "It's been eight years, and soon enough for the man to find someone."

"They said nothing to me when I came this morning." He ran through the women in his mind, dismissing Bettina as already married. The new girl seemed too young. That left only Jane.

Parson laughed. "It's a bit early for that, and I seem to remember you took your time as well. Though not as heavy in the purse as you are, the boys grew used to the benefits of your courting. We'd send one of us for rolls every so often. I don't think any of us caught on for a bit to how Fitz would be quick to volunteer, but the way he lingers at the task is unmistakable. Only look how long it took him to arrive this morning."

Henry wondered if he'd been the cause today, Fitz delaying when he saw who stood within the bakery. If he had, though, the rolls would have been well hidden when Fitz arrived at the station—or left for the shop girls—not out there in the man's hands for him to spy.

"What can I say?" Fitz shrugged, the last crumbs gone from his fingers. "I am a fool for a woman who can bake, and that Jane sure is pleasant on the eyes."

For all his funning, Fitzwilliam had a serious streak and fierce dedication. Henry marveled that so flighty a girl as Jane could capture his interest. But then, as Parson said, it had been eight years. In that time, Sam had grown from a precocious child into a budding young woman. He'd noticed Jane's apparent maturity himself.

Henry gripped the other man's shoulder. "I won't be the one to warn you off as you once did for me. She's a good woman, that Jane, and deserves a good man."

Dark red swallowed Fitz's expression. "And I'm not good enough for her?"

Henry frowned. "No. You misunderstand. I think you're perfect for her, though what Cooper will do if those set to protecting the streets treat his bakery as a marriage mart I cannot say."

Fitz relaxed, a rueful smile replacing his anger. "He'll be happier with my choice. Jane won't be leaving the bakery."

"So you've spoken to her?" Jim asked.

The smile broadened into a grin. "Spoken to her and her parents both. I have their blessing."

The table erupted in congratulations, this news grand enough even to distract them from the pastries.

Henry added his to the mix then withdrew, knowing he had become nothing more than an interloper as much as he enjoyed their company. Still, it brought back memories of his own courting days, both the teasing, and how Fitz and Parson made sure he had Lily's best interests in mind. Nostalgia pulled at him for those times though they'd been no simpler than where he found himself now.

"And how goes the politics?"

Parson's question drew Henry out of his thoughts, the lead officer having stepped free of the crowd to join him.

Henry shrugged. "I'd like to believe I'm making some progress, but it seems as many are set against me as for me, and many of those who support only do so silently from the shadows. It's almost as though I never spoke to them that first time. There's no mention of the points I raised unless it is to misinterpret what I said and use that to strengthen fears. If I didn't know better, I'd think someone deliberately worked to undermine my position."

He hadn't meant to unload his worries on Parson, but he'd been holding so much in, and Henry had no one else he could trust to listen out here. Lily would have soothed his concerns, but she'd made it clear his place was in London. The worst of it came from how he knew she was right. He could no longer stand aside and let this tragedy remain.

"That is all too likely if there were anything to gain from confining the Naturals. I can't imagine just protecting possessions to be enough of a reason though." Parson stilled. "It could be someone who has turned his child in and cannot face the possibility of it being the wrong choice."

They shared a pained look, then Parson laughed.

"No. Guilt might make a man reluctant, but it wouldn't make him fight. Not when compared to the chance of recovering his child. Only greed would drive one to block something clearly right."

Henry pondered Parson's words. They felt true.

He had grown so frustrated he saw opposition where there was only reluctance. With nothing to gain, why mount a full resistance? His words had nothing more than rumor and history to weigh against them, both aspects he could wear down given time.

"All right, boys. Enough with the hanging about. You're not paid to rest on your bums," Parson called to the others who had gone back to enjoying their treats with Parson distracted.

"And I should be off as well," Henry told his friends. "I have minds and hearts to change if the laws are to be built on a foundation firmer than greed and fear."

A chorus of well wishes and good hopes followed him to the door as the others gathered up their gear for the patrol ahead of them.

Henry's step felt lighter and the smile on his face drew greetings from those he passed as he strode off to his lodgings. Fitz reminded him of the earlier days when he'd courted Lily, showing dedication and persistence enough to win a battle he hadn't known the extent of until almost too late. If he could earn the trust and love of his wife, surely he could ease the fears of those with the ability to change laws that lacked any precedence to support them.

*I*N HER FOCUS ON BELL, Lily had neglected to tend her feet, making the trip down the stairs just as treacherous as the way up. She chose to endure rather than create another delay between Bell and a need for food stronger than the draw of Sam's mechanicals.

The grip on her hand grew tighter as they neared the kitchen, but Bell made not a sound. When she spoke, her diction came clear, but Lily noticed she'd be just as likely to keep silent. Whether this was a new aspect since being cast out or an old one, Lily had no way to tell.

"Go get some preserves from the cellar," Cook called to one of the maids as they stepped in the door. "And be careful with it. Just because summer is coming on fast and the berries are ripening is no cause to waste either jar or contents."

Bell pressed a hand to her mouth to stifle what Lily suspected to be a giggle from how the girl's body shivered, the result of nerves rather than humor most likely what with Cook in mid-scold.

Lily tugged on their bound hands and crossed to the table where she waved Bell to one of the stools.

"We were wondering if you had anything to spare," Lily said to Cook's back where she rolled out some form of pastry.

"Oh!" A puff of flour rose into the air like a smoke cloud as Cook jumped in surprise.

The giggle escaped Bell then, a sound full of joy rather than fear.

Cook glanced from Lily to Bell, one flour-coated hand pressed to the top of her apron. "Mistress, you startled me sneaking in here like that. A body could have mistaken you for your sister just then." She waved her free hand in Bell's direction, sending more flour about the room. "And who is our little guest?"

Had there been fear or anger in the tone, Lily suspected Bell would have shrunk away. Instead, the girl gave a broad smile, clearly having spent more than her share of time in the kitchen of her own home.

"Her name is Bell. She's an orphan come to stay with us for a while. I hope you will welcome her."

Cook gave a headshake though her smile softened the rejection. "What kind of stray will you be bringing in next?"

Their conversation had drawn three of the others, Abigail among them.

Lily made quick introductions, but the four women stood on the other side of the table seemingly at a loss.

Then Cook straightened as though coming awake. "An orphan you don't say? I'll bet she has an empty stomach in that case." She leaned on the table until her face came level with Bell's. "Would you like something to eat?"

Bell nodded with such vigor she almost unseated herself, and the rest fell to laughing.

"It will be nice having a young one about once again, especially one with a good appetite."

As though the statement had been a sign they were to get back to work, the maids paused only long enough to give Bell and Lily quick curtsies before they scattered. Cook moved to her table, quickly slicing up the dough and placing it on a baking tray.

"I'll have Susan bring some of yesterday's biscuits I was saving for a crust. These scones need more time than I suspect little Bell is eager to wait."

Just then, the kitchen girl appeared and almost dropped the precious jar of preserves as she took in Bell's presence. At the last moment, Susan regained her grip long enough to push the jar onto the kitchen table.

"Who's this then?" the kitchen girl asked.

Bell looked up from the jar and said, "I'm Bell."

Susan gave a broad smile and stuck out a hand, revealing she'd spent much too much time among the stable boys.

Bell stared at the appendage as though unsure what to do with it.

"Susan," Lily cut in, "do you know where Cook has kept the day olds?"

The kitchen girl jerked her attention to Lily and flushed a dark red. "Of course, mistress." This time she remembered a curtsy if one as awkward as any from Abigail.

Lily watched Bell's gaze sweep the room, pausing each time something caught her eye. The first seemed to be the old water pump, and Lily tensed, knowing more than a few of the staff would be nervous to learn a Natural had come under this roof a second time. Though Kate seemed the only one with an active dislike, Lily understood all too well how these had accepted Sam despite her nature, not because of it.

Then Lily realized the girl gave just as much attention to the row of ceramic mugs and realized the pump could have a very different meaning.

Susan laid a plate of hardened biscuits onto the table, the stoneware giving a solid thunk.

Bell swiveled back, her full attention on the food before her.

"I'll just get a knife to cut them and a spoon for the preserves," Susan said, already turning to take on the task.

"Please fetch Bell some water as well. I doubt the tea is ready this early."

Cook laughed, her ears focused even as she worked the last of the dough. "The staff tea's hot and ready, mistress. Can't see as how the girl will object."

At this point Susan returned with a knife and made short work of the biscuits, giving one a thick spread of the fruit before presenting it to Bell.

"Thank you," the little girl murmured before taking one delicate nip after another from the biscuit, hardly stopping long enough to chew.

"You'd best slow down or you'll give yourself a stomachache," Cook said as she lifted a second tray to carry to the ovens.

Bell glanced to Lily who gave her an encouraging nod just as tea appeared at both their elbows courtesy of Susan.

"A drink is just the thing." Lily tipped some cream into hers and did the same for Bell.

Susan added two more small plates so Bell would have some place to put her food down while she drank and Lily could join in the meal as well. She then went about her work as did the others, but Lily saw how they glanced this way often, full of natural curiosity.

Just as Sunshine had first caused an uproar but now grew fat on the treats they slipped him, Lily suspected Bell would be quick to find her place in the household. Lily had not lied in calling the staff nice. She only hoped Bell's appeal would be enough to help them forgive Lily the secret should they discover how Bell came to find them.

The longer Bell kept her nature hidden, though, the better. While these might forgive and understand, Lily knew Kate would be all the harder to convince just as she'd been with the kitten. But if that scamp could win her over despite depositing kills in the house, Bell's adorable features and polite manners could very well succeed even with the hardest member of the staff.

Had Sam been more of a Samantha, perhaps her nature would have proved less of a barrier for Kate. Lily suspected the boyish carelessness as much at fault as any transformations her sister might have performed, while Bell showed no signs of wanting to wander about getting in trouble.

A smile teased Lily's lips as she tucked her feet further under her skirts. Between the two of them, she had more claim to the title of trouble with her feet still untended, and how she gallivanted around the house in her robe and nightdress. She'd spent so much time attempting to curtail such behavior in her sister, but now it gave Lily a sense of kinship with the absent Sam.

Somehow, Lily knew Sam would be the first to approve of the decision to give Bell a home. Her sister had ever been generous, even if on occasion that meant with items she had no claim to.

*H*ENRY REACHED HIS TOWN HOUSE some time later in the morning, but not so late that society would have stirred. He'd grown used to country hours, and he hadn't kept to society's habits even when in London thanks to being a police officer.

Still, the walk had done him good.

Seeing the London streets stir to life first with the maids about their chores, then the street vendors calling their wares up to windows newly opened to let in a breeze reminded him of his purpose. How many of these goodly folk had made the hard choice to risk the law or tear their hearts asunder? And if not themselves, surely they knew of someone who had lost a child or sibling to the asylums.

Whether he acted for Sam or the many faceless Naturals in hiding, he could not let mere frustration stand in his way. Not when there was so much to gain should he succeed.

Henry laughed as he mounted the steps two at a time. Not should but when. If he could win Lily's hand with Sam at risk, the hearts of Parliament should be easy to sway, in comparison at least.

His housekeeper met him at the door, her dark hands wringing together.

"What is it, Bessie?" The woman had been elevated to run the small staff when Mrs. Thompson retired, a decision Henry had little cause to regret. Normally nothing would have flustered her.

"A man came for you. Said it was urgent. He wouldn't believe me when I told him you weren't at home. Thought I was trying to keep your privacy or some such. He became quite belligerent, he did."

Henry clapped a hand on the woman's shoulder even as his mind spun with what the news could have been. "I apologize in his stead, Bessie. You should not have had to suffer such just because most keep to London hours and so would have been present whether receiving or not."

Then a thought came that weakened his knees, and he leaned a bit too heavily on his housekeeper from how her eyes widened.

"Is he still here? Did he leave a message? Tell me it wasn't about my wife." The only way it could have been was if she'd taken a turn for the worse and with him so far away.

Bessie shook her head vigorously, a gentle smile on her broad lips. "No, my lord. You needn't worry for your lovely wife. This man said he'd come from Parliament.

A different jolt thrust through him at that, one bringing energy where worry had stolen it from him.

"What did he say?" This time eagerness rather than fear colored his demand.

Bessie scowled. "He didn't think I could hold a message. When I wouldn't fetch you from whatever cupboard he decided I'd tucked you into, he left a letter with no hint as to its contents."

"And the letter is...?" Henry encouraged, holding back a chuckle.

The man most likely thought a written missive proof against Bessie's curiosity, seeing only her dark skin and servant's apron instead of the intelligence in her eyes.

He'd taught her to read himself when tutors filled his life. His parents encouraged the practice, though whether for his benefit in learning by teaching or hers, he would never know. Still, Bessie's elevation to housekeeper had been well deserved.

Bessie gave a quiet harrumph and turned to pluck the missive from the letter basket by the door. She held it pinched between two fingers as she handed it over, Henry discovering the reason when it rested in his palm.

A seal bound the seam together, blocking Bessie's curiosity in the only way possible. She'd taken to helping him sort the correspondence and would read everything that came in before sending it on to his country estate with the appropriate speed. But she'd never break open a sealed note. Not without his explicit permission.

"Thank you," he murmured even as he carried it toward his study. "I'm sure it's nothing more than another delay," he called over his shoulder, as much to calm his own eagerness as to relieve her need to know.

When he reached his desk, the seal gave way beneath the pressure of his paper knife. He scanned the contents with the eagerness of a young boy hoping to go to Eton.

He read the note a second time to be sure of the import, but it remained the same.

An opening had come up unexpectedly in the schedule for this very day, hence the urgency. He would be allowed to address Parliament for a second time at last.

After dashing a quick note of acceptance, he sought out Bessie once again.

"I've another chance to address them but only if this note is received before they give the opportunity to someone else. Can you send it on for me?"

She gave him a broad smile, confident he worked to help people even if she'd had her doubts about those he championed now. "Don't you worry. I'll have this in that nasty man's fingers faster than he can find a new reason to scorn me."

Henry laughed at the thought of the poor clerk who'd been foolish enough to get on her bad side.

"You take such good care of me," he said aloud.

"We do our best, my lord."

Still chuckling, Henry returned to his study to get down to work. He spared a quick prayer for the man who had fallen ill to create this opening, hoping the illness would be brief, but most of his attention focused on the puzzle of what to say. He had only a few short hours to prepare, and he'd given little thought to his next approach, waiting for the chance rather than working ahead as he should have done.

As much as he might regret the fact now, dwelling on his lack provided no assistance. Instead, Parson's words rose from memory.

What if there were something to gain? Not from continuing this unjust path but from changing it? Surely that would catch the attention of those in both Houses.

15

After breakfast, Lily enlisted Abigail's aid to open up Samantha's room once again and move all the old, outgrown clothing back into her sister's cabinets. The early morning and unaccustomed exertion soon caught up with her, though, and she left the maid to help Bell settle, reminding the little girl to keep her secret in a quiet whisper.

Lily returned well rested and better for having taken the time to scrub the dirt from the soles of her feet, her shoes now safely donned despite the way they pinched the cuts she'd suffered.

A quick word to Cook, and a picnic had been prepared. Bell might be more ladylike than Sam ever was, but no young child could resist the urge to run about in an open field.

Sunshine had taken to the little girl more than any of the others. Lily watched the two gambol through the flowers, Bell stopping to pluck one after another as she crafted a crown to match the one already on her head. Laughter danced over to Lily on the breeze while she smiled to see the difference a single day could make.

Had anyone suggested Bell were mute and scared of her own shadow now, the description would seem far-fetched, and yet that's exactly what she'd been in the early morning hours. Two meals later, a new dress, and a room of her own left no sign of that terrified child.

As though aware of Lily's scrutiny, Bell hopped and skipped her way to the tree under which Lily sat on a spread blanket.

"I have a present for you," the girl said when she neared.

Lily smiled and put out a hand to receive the second flower crown.

Instead, Bell dug into the pocket of her skirt and pulled out something that sparkled in the bright noon sun.

Lily's shoulders tensed even before the girl dropped the gift into her open palm.

"A mechanical dog." In Sam's voice, the words would have been filled with awe, but Lily's gut churned at the sight, and her naming held more curse than blessing. Perhaps she'd been wrong about Bell's control and only hunger kept the knack weak.

"This isn't hiding your talents."

Bell cocked her head to one side, confusion pinching her brows together. Then she laughed and shook her head. "It has no life. It's just a thing I built for you."

As the girl spoke, Lily realized the machine had not moved since being placed on her hand, unlike any of Sam's creations. It lay there, still and silent, a mere echo of what it could be.

Bell frowned all the harder. "Don't you like it? I know it has no energy to it, but that will come in time."

"How did you do this?" Lily ignored the question and the statement to follow as well. Sam had always taken something with energy, as Bell called it, already present.

A shrug looked to be the only answer Lily would get, then Bell shrugged a second time.

"I like to work with my hands. I always have. I used to help Mother in the kitchen, but also to make toys for the other children. They're not special at first, and sometimes they never become so. They are just things I made. Like this."

She held out the flower crown Lily had been expecting for her gift, but with none of the delight in her expression as when she'd given the toy.

Lily suspected her response, not the different construction, stood at fault for the change.

Now she understood just how this girl had come to be tossed out of her home. Children would delight to discover their favorite toys come to life. Not so their parents, or the local constables.

"I thought Sam had packed everything away." Her voice sounded faint even to Lily's own ears.

Bell's gaze turned inexorably toward the workshop though it wasn't visible from where they were. "She did. Everything special. I made the toy out of spare parts I found scattered in her room."

Lily sighed, wanting nothing more than to share in the delight Bell had first offered, to encourage her mundane talents where she could not the other, but special or not, little mechanical devices cropping up would raise questions they needed to avoid.

"You cannot go around making things like that, Bell. They'll give away your secret even before they come to life. You've already had to leave one home. You should know better than to risk this one."

Her voice had turned hard with the fear of losing Bell as she had Sam, but remorse filled her at the sight of Bell's stricken features.

"I'm sorry," she said, realizing only too late how harsh her words would be to the little girl's ears. Fear of discovery offered little excuse when this girl had lost both home and family through her generosity of spirit.

Bell stared at her feet, returned to the feral child Lily had brought in from the workshop doors.

Lily stretched out a hand to comfort but let it drop. How many times had she crushed Sam's spirit in the same way? Keeping a Natural safe meant more than avoiding the notice of the law. It meant nurturing a vibrant life when fear would all too quickly beat it down. Exhaustion swept over her, its weight as heavy as the guilt she bore.

"We should go back now," Lily said into the crushing silence. She cursed the necessity and her blindness to the cost, but had little choice if she were to protect Bell from the same fate that had haunted Sam.

Bell quietly helped Lily pack up the remains of their lunch, saying nothing when Lily thrust the ill-timed gift out of sight into a pocket. The little girl said nothing at all, her silence as damning as any amount of protest.

They rose and folded the blanket, Lily tucking it under one arm while Bell took up the basket.

At the last moment, Bell slid her fingers into Lily's free hand. "I promise I will not do that again. I will make nothing at all. I would never want to bring you harm. You've been nothing but kind."

Though Lily forced a smile to her lips, her heart ached for a promise so necessary and yet holding such pain. "It's just that we must be careful. We can't give people a reason to suspect."

A solemn nod came as her only answer, but Lily gave Bell's hand a reassuring squeeze. They set off for the manor house at more than the dragging pace Lily had expected.

Harsh laws cost them so much, and none paid a stiffer price than those born with a special gift and denied the right

to use it. If only Henry's efforts found success, she could revoke any scolding and let Bell be the person she'd been born
to be rather than a shadow of same, unable to show the world
her light.

HE MEMBERS OF BOTH HOUSES seemed in grand
spirits. From the comments Henry overheard as he
made his way to his seat, many had been at a splendid boxing
match between two fierce combatants. He didn't know if this
would make them more willing to hear him out or too rowdy
to listen, but Henry knew he'd found an argument to appeal to
every one of them.

His fears of a rowdy group proved true with the early orders of business, but at the same time, if he could redirect
some of that passion to his purpose, they'd revise the Natural
laws this very day. Henry picked up his sheaf of papers, a mix
of notes and speech fragments, and made his way down to the
floor.

"Come to tell us reformed monster stories once again, Stapleton?"

Though he flashed a smile in the direction of the call,
Henry had no idea who had spoken. Still, let them voice their
doubts now. It only gave him a better understanding of his
opposition.

After the usual address, which was met with many catcalls,
Henry leaned both hands on the Dispatch Box and swept the
room with his gaze. His very silence brought the whole of
Parliament to an expectant pause into which he dropped the
key to his position.

"The time of industry has seen much change, change that has benefited us here the most of all. With the new rules of productivity, both wealth and position rests in the hands of those capable of shoring up an economy rife with problems. We are rebuilding Mother England from the wreckage of wastrel years into a strong, robust nation."

The seats creaked and the room thundered as the members cheered a sentiment stronger here than in any other part. Those who could not contribute had been stripped of their voice in Parliament if not their titles, while the untitled Commons had long strove to reward hard labor.

Henry waited for them to settle once again before he twisted them on the hook. "These rules of industry hold that every able-bodied person must labor, do they not?"

This response came slower as they started to question his point.

"Why is it then we waste some among us who have unique talents that could be turned to the cause of industry?" Henry continued. "If even a few Naturals can be brought to honest labor, just imagine the advances they could secure. Are we to be the first among all nations to realize this asset? Or the last."

Again he waited, though he could see this argument reached many more ears than ever his moral position had. Fear held sway over kindness, but in the name of avarice, many would undertake tasks that might risk their very lives.

He pushed down a smile at the realization the description held true even for the old wealth and titles among them. More titles had been awarded survivors of the battlefield than ever for assistance to the crown in less deadly circumstances.

"Just how would you suggest we go about this, then?" a man called from where the Commons found their places. "And who would be responsible for these monsters?"

Henry raised both hands, not in surrender but in a request for patience. "There is much still to discuss, and choices to be made before the Naturals can be tested against the needs of industry. In advance of any such endeavors, though, the laws that hold Naturals as monsters—good and criminal alike— must be torn down. Let us take the first step to identify those in our care who are capable, who have not been thrust so far out of society as to revert to a feral state, and mend the tears caused by unjust laws."

The grumbles his words brought forth were as many as any in support.

Henry realized he had veered too close to his original argument, and worse, the asylum he had been to would have no good examples to draw on if Parson's account held truth as he felt sure it must. If the only Naturals they could find were as far gone as the man he'd delivered eight years earlier, even those in agreement would lose faith.

"It's those not yet confined who are of the most interest," Henry said, speaking rapidly. "These are men and women, children as well, who are capable of remaining hidden among us and yet capable of so much more. It's these to whom we must appeal because they will be the ones with the control necessary to offer skills and profit."

An older lord rose, one who had weathered the low times like Henry's own family so still had enough wealth to retain his spot. "And just how do you suggest we discover these 'hidden Naturals' if they are so capable of conforming to the rules of society?"

Henry shot him a grateful smile though he knew the man intended scorn as much as the Parliament messenger had to Bessie.

"The only possible way is to revoke the Natural laws. If they are not fugitives who will be captured as soon as they admit their nature, they have no cause to hide."

The room erupted at that, some crying foul, others questioning his sanity, and still more shouting in his stead.

Henry knew he'd made an argument with strength. He knew as well he'd made more than one enemy this day. Though he couldn't understand why, some members held strong against him regardless of his path.

He glanced from one to the next, remembering the letters he'd received discouraging this effort. Those who were not arguing with their fellows sent him glares from beneath lowered brows. They didn't seem the types to quake at the thought of Naturals roaming the streets. More likely they'd consider such beneath their attention. And yet he had no reason to doubt their opposition, and no hope of changing their minds.

By the time quiet had been restored, his address had ended with no decisions made. Henry had to comfort himself with the knowledge he'd won over a few and led even more to consider what they'd previously rejected outright. He refused to give up hope in this cause as much as he had to accept there were some he'd never convince, those who had written to condemn him among them.

How many would return to their homes this night to consider for the first time the waste of casting aside such talents when even a slight possibility existed they could be taught to turn their skills to the benefit of all. More specifically, to the benefit of their sponsors, all of whom, no doubt, would come from the ranks of Parliament itself.

With that he had to be satisfied. He'd made great strides today, for all it might seem as though nothing had changed. Next time, perhaps, he'd be able to bring things to a vote.

16

Henry set off for home early the next morning, his mood buoyed by the letters and cards he'd received in the night. Though he should have stayed to return the cards, often with corners turned to show a wished for meeting, he could not keep this response from Lily.

Last time, he'd reached the manor filled with frustrations and fears. She, more than any other, deserved to share in this realization of his best hopes. He'd delayed leaving only long enough to write up a letter for each of those expressing interest in talking with him, explaining that he'd been called home to pressing business and would be happy to speak with them on his return.

Henry left the few letters from his opponents on his desk and instructed Bessie to hold any more of either type. With progress to be made, he couldn't linger at the country estate, but neither would he stay here and tell Lily how the Natural laws now quaked in fear for their future with a simple note.

The stables appeared before him much sooner than expected, the lathered state of his horse chiding him for an eagerness that kept them racing forward where a carriage would have stopped. Henry swung down and gave the beast a pat on the neck in gratitude as he called out for one of the stable boys.

In the short time before assistance appeared, Henry had already undone his saddlebags and thrown them over one shoulder.

"Give him a cool down walk, if you please. He's earned his oats, but I wouldn't want to make him ill."

"Yes, my lord," the boy said with a crisp salute.

Henry shook his head, wondering whether a brother in the army or a nearby troop set the boy to this form. They'd have to take care, or they'd lose him to the starry-eyed hopes of a battlefield.

As he mounted the steps at a run, every thought but those of his wife fell away.

"Lily," he called, "I'm home."

Abigail came from the kitchen, red-faced with eyes sparkling, before he'd even reached the sitting room.

"She's not here, my lord."

Henry halted so quickly he fought a stumble. "Where is she then?"

His question came out a sharp bark, and some of her light dimmed.

She pressed her lips together, most likely against a scold though she'd never shown such assurance, then said, "She's picnicking by the large maple."

Henry stared at her, realizing after the fact how his jaw had fallen open.

"Picnicking?" A moment too late, he remembered the request that Kate continue the practice, though he'd half-expected to discover nothing had come of it, especially with the lady's maid banished to her father's home.

Her cheer returned as she grinned at him. "Yes, my lord. She's out there with Bell."

The name triggered no connections in his mind, but he didn't bother to ask as he dropped his bags and turned back the way he'd come. He knew Lily had been looking better, but to make such an effort all on her own could only mean a significant improvement. Though he had not allowed himself to consider how poorly she'd been this winter, the relief threatened to overwhelm him.

Echoes of Abigail's laughter followed him out the door, but he didn't care. Good news seemed to flock around him as though their difficulties had finally ended.

Sure enough, he spied Lily stretched on a rug, her gaze directed to the fields so she did not see him. Henry chose not to distract her until he dropped to her side, gathering his surprised wife into his arms.

"Henry! You're back and so soon?"

Her words curved up at the end and a frown threatened her brow, but he smoothed it with a kiss. "Not for long, but I had to see how you were doing. Here I've been sick with worry in London, and you're skipping about the fields."

"Hardly that," Lily said with a laugh, "Though I'm feeling better than I have in years."

He glanced around the field, remembering the cause of her restoration at the same time as realizing the kitten must have held her gaze.

Time froze, though, when he found the true target. "Who is she?"

The question came out harder than he had intended, but it seemed he had no way to recognize this Bell. One of the village children come to prey on Lily's generosity, no doubt.

Without realizing it, he'd half risen to confront the child, but Lily drew him down.

"Her name is Bell. I have taken her in."

She explained in quick sentences how she'd come by this child, and Henry's concerns grew with each one.

"I haven't been able to learn her full name, or that of her parents. How they must worry about her. I can't imagine the pain it caused for them to set her to run, but it's clear enough they loved her greatly. They would not have cast her out unless to save her."

Henry's darker thoughts melted away at this last. Lily had stood ready to throw aside everything she'd worked for when it seemed Sam would be threatened by discovery. He could not expect her to turn away from another little girl in the same circumstances.

"I've considered whether to ask about," she continued, un-aware of his conflicted thoughts, "but though she's clearly a rural child, she's also educated. Who knows how long she's been roaming on her own. Trying to find her parents would only raise questions and draw the wrong attention."

He froze at that, realizing how much the attention could cost them, especially now. "You say the workshop drew her. She's probably been sheltered by the very rarity of mechanical devices out here in the country, though there are enough to have brought her to trouble even so."

Lily nodded then. "She has either a weaker gift or much more control than Sam ever did. She even crafts things from nothing. Not living devices, but simple toys."

The delight in her expression gave him pause.

The kitten had restored her purpose, but this girl had clear-ly done that and more. Though there were reasons enough not to inquire after parents who were likely under surveillance, Henry knew as he said a quick word of agreement his motiva-tions came from a much more selfish root.

He would do anything to bring Lily back to health, even if it meant letting her adopt another Natural when he too might be subject to scrutiny, even knowing the child's parents must mourn for her as much as Lily did for Sam. If this Bell brought light into his wife's eyes, she would have every protection he could offer.

"I think it's time I met this new member of our family, don't you?"

The grin she shot his direction before calling Bell over only strengthened his conviction. They'd hidden Sam out here for eight years, and in this case, his staff didn't even know the girl's nature. They could keep Bell safe, and once he changed the laws, they could even help her find her family once again just as Sam could be brought home.

WHEN BELL CAME OVER, LILY could see the hesitation in the girl's eyes, perhaps recognizing the remnants of Henry's police officer stance.

"It's all right. This is my Henry. I've told you about him before. He will not harm you."

Bell looked up, and her brows pinched together. "You won't make me go, will you?"

Lily thought his frown would have scared the little girl away, but perhaps Bell could see his anger was directed at others even before he spoke.

"No, child. I only wanted to meet you. You are welcome here and safe."

Her eyes widened then as she stared at Lily. "He knows?"

Lily nodded. "Yes. He knows, but Henry alone. No one else can."

"So I won't make him anything either. I promised."

Lily felt Henry's gaze fall on her, but kept her attention focused on Bell as she smiled. "It's good to keep your promises. Why don't you go back and play some more? Henry can keep me company."

Bell gave Henry a curtsy as elegant as any at London balls, or so Lily guessed from her husband's laugh, then scampered off to rejoin Sunshine. The cat had not deigned to come any closer.

"She's very different from Sam, isn't she? A little lady."

Lily slapped his shoulder in protest. "Not a fair comparison when I had the raising of Sam on my own. And yes, she has much better manners and ways than my sister ever attained."

He brushed a finger down Lily's cheek as if to trace a tear she refused to shed. "I did not indicate a preference, just recognition. Somehow I doubt she'd be willing to wrestle with me."

Lily jerked around to face him fully, having kept her gaze on Bell's retreat until then. "You wrestled with Sam? No wonder I had little success in making a lady of her. You were too busy encouraging her boyish ways behind my back."

Henry shrugged rather than admit what was clearly the truth. At least his failures could only help her sister now.

"So tell me of London. Surely you cannot have finished your business there so soon."

"I came to check on you, love, as I said, but as much to tell you the results of my latest approach." His gaze drifted out to the field, clearly watching her foundling.

"What were those, pray tell?" she asked.

His lips firmed before he let out a deep sigh. "I found the way into the members' hearts is through banknotes rather than appealing to their conscience. More are willing to entertain the possibility with the chance Naturals could use their gifts for industry, and their sponsor's profit, of course."

Again he turned to look at Bell, and Lily smiled.

"She's much more able to control her knack, and she builds things even when there's no bout in sight. Bell would be a perfect example to hold before them."

Henry shook his head, rejecting the idea without any further consideration. "Don't you see? The reason I'm able to approach this topic is because Sam has gone away. With Bell here, I have as much cause to stay silent as any of those who responded kindly to my first request."

He sighed again, a pensive look in his eyes as he stared out to where Bell and Sunshine danced in the field.

Lily put a hand on his thigh and gave a light squeeze. "You do not have to worry about Bell. Don't give up now when you're making progress. Only you, I, and Bell know her nature. She does nothing to draw suspicion, either. When she makes a promise, she not only does so with good intentions but with the ability to hold to it. As you yourself saw, she is not Sam."

"If she slips even once, my motives would become suspect. They know my background, and it's the only reason they do not scrutinize me further. They know I've put at least one Natural behind the asylum walls."

Lily flinched, unable to help herself even now with that time far behind them. The asylum had been a nightmare threatening her for far too long.

Henry caught her hand and rubbed his fingers across her palm. "I only remind you to explain. If the punishment falls on my head, so be it. I believe in what I'm doing. But I cannot chance you, and now Bell, suffering for my purpose."

Lily pushed aside her fears to squeeze his fingers tight. "Don't you see? If you back down now, having made some inroads, you will be harming Bell more than anything we risk. She's young. She misses her parents, and she's yet to be twisted by the false beliefs about her nature. If you can make this change, she may never end up dreaming of all the things she cannot have and cannot do as Sam clearly did."

She glanced toward the little girl, as caught up in her vision of the future as she'd hoped to capture Henry's imagination. "Bell could be an Englishwoman like any other, but only if you stay strong and true to your purpose. Think of how it would look should you step into the shadows. You'd be all but saying those who opposed your first attempt were right. That you had misjudged the Naturals. You would be condemning them all the harsher for having once stood up for their concerns."

Lily stopped to draw in a deep breath, but neither freed his hand nor shifted her gaze from his dear face.

When Henry shook his head, some of the energy drained out of her. She slumped, knowing her choice to bring Bell into their lives would cost every single Natural their strongest advocate.

Callused fingertips brushed her chin, bringing her gaze up to meet Henry's. "You're right, my love. If I shy away now, no one else will take up the cause in my stead. Even the members already counting their coins would have little to gain in standing against those who oppose me so fiercely. This new approach did nothing to change the minds of my opponents. However, it worked on the majority of members who swayed in neither direction before this."

A smile curved her lips as she met the determination in his gaze. "My Henry. Always the crusader not only in the call of Queen and Country but also in that of the smallest among us. I should have known you would not give in so easily, but you should be in London still. Those minds you have started to change won't stand firm against your opponents without you there to shore them up."

"Are you so quick to be rid of me?" he asked with a chuckle.

Lily pulled her hand free only to shove his chest with both palms. "Be gone with you. You have more important duties than sitting vigil at my side."

She could have kicked herself as soon as the words left her mouth. He went still, the features that had been so relaxed becoming pinched with worry.

"I thought you were doing better. You certainly seem to be, and here you are out on a picnic without me to carry you home."

Lily shook her head as hard as she could, strands of hair slapping him. "I am. I thought at first it would not last, but the summer warmth has come early, and I feel stronger than I have in years. My hopes have been crushed too many times to count on this, but having Sunshine then Bell to dote on seems to have proven quite the restorative."

Her voice softened as she added, "Go on to London. Serve your greater purpose without the distraction of worrying about me. I fear I'll still be present when you return and will expect your full attention then."

He mock scowled at her tease. "You had better be. There's no one else on this earth I want to share the news of my victory with. Just look at how I raced here to tell you of a little progress in that direction."

"So sure you'll succeed then?" Lily chided, though her lips twitched with her true response.

"With your support, even from a good day's distance, how can I not be? My cause is just though I cloak it in yards of gold, and my words no longer fall on deaf ears. You keep Bell safe, and I'll make sure she'll never have to fear again."

Lily smiled up at him, basking in his confidence until the silence between them grew into a different tension all together, one they could not address with Bell watching.

"Well, what are you waiting for?" she asked as much to dispel the desire to feel his lips on hers as to continue the tease.

Henry frowned. "Do not become a scold, my love. Do I not at least deserve a meal before you set me back on the road? If nothing else, my horse needs a good rest."

Lily shrugged. "You have other horses, but I suppose one night away will bring no harm."

He drew her close for a quick peck that satisfied neither of them. "And it has done much good. I'll return renewed with your faith and relieved of my worries. I'll handily battle every doubt while keeping my opponents at bay, all because I had a moment to enjoy your company."

A rumble of thunder gave weight to his statement, and Henry laughed.

"Call your new friend home, Lily. I fear the rain will take away your comfortable rest. We must get the both of you to shelter."

She rose and called for Bell before helping him pack up the remains of their meal, her heart swollen with love. He ever thought of others before himself and willingly provided shelter even when doing so brought the risk of punishment on his own head. Though the pain of a thorough soaking was nothing, he'd chanced much worse since he'd talked to her that first day in Cooper's Bakery. If ever the Naturals needed aid, no better man existed than Henry to give it.

17

After a wonderful two days in Bell's company, marveling at the joy and laughter her presence brought to his household, Henry mounted a different horse from his stables and headed back to London. This child had little in common with Sam, with her ladylike manners and soft giggles, but her effect on Lily remained the same. Perhaps their differences allowed for the relief, as pain still shadowed his wife's features whenever her sister came to mind.

The thought sobered him as he straightened in the saddle, keeping to a quick pace but not as punishing a speed as he had on the way down. The two girls had one other similarity, one he'd do best not to forget.

How long before Lily's happiness turned sharp and strove against her?

He'd been so sure that caring for Sam had kept his wife from healing. Now, instead of worrying about someone discovering her sister at the manor, Lily had Sam out who knew where, and a Natural at home as well so the old fears would soon return.

His knees tightened reflexively, sending him to London all the faster.

Henry had it within him to make both those worries vanish for Lily and all others in a similar state. If he drove Parliament to change the Natural laws, he could ensure Bell never had to face losing someone again the way she had lost her parents.

As to Sam, where now they sought any mention or rumor of a Natural, unable to ask questions, then they could seek for Lily's sister overtly. They could bring Sam home. Home to a place where she could be herself.

The miles vanished beneath shod hooves as Henry contemplated his next moves.

He had first to return all those cards he'd received, requesting meetings where he could secure them. Perhaps he'd find allies among them ready to work out a plan of action instead of just more talk.

The day grew bright and cheery, though the sun did not burn down hot enough to cause stains to leak through to his jacket. For once, it felt as though everything moved in the right direction, taking them forward toward a better future.

The kitten and Bell might have eased Lily's sorrows, but nothing would have more of an impact on his lovely wife than seeing her sister to safety, or even better, back at the manor with them. He vowed to do everything in his reach to bring that about before winter set in and threatened to take his Lily away.

For once, the oath didn't ring hollow. It might take hard work, but he'd never been afraid of getting his hands dirty for the right cause. He stood on the brink of winning freedom for Sam, Bell, and every other of their nature. Of freeing anyone who'd ever loved a Natural as well—parents, brothers, sisters, and even strangers who came across lost children in the fields.

Henry understood his brother's eagerness to stand up in Parliament for the first time. He'd thought glory drove Robert, but now he knew the emotion much more complicated and more like the urge he'd had to become a police officer than he'd ever suspected.

"I'll do more than just warm the seat that should have been yours, Robert. You wanted to bring about a better society. I plan to bring equality even to Naturals."

Only his horse heard the words given to a man many years gone. The animal tossed its head as though in agreement and stretched its legs a little further so each canter took them that much closer to London and Parliament where Henry swore to make good on his promise.

*T*HE DAYS AT THE ESTATE quickly settled into a routine, one with little need to be careful of Lily. With the warmth of summer approaching and Bell's company, not to mention Sunshine's antics, Lily felt stronger every morning and still had energy by the end of every day.

She tried not to let herself hope for a true recovery. She'd long given up on the possibility. But for now, at least, it seemed she'd been given a reprieve.

They'd been sitting in the conservatory all morning, working on some stitchery. Bell had wanted to give the staff something for their willingness to embrace her just as she'd made a gift for Lily. The idea of handkerchiefs with initials stitched carefully at the corners had come from Lily. She'd worried about what her foundling might decide on without guidance, as much as she enjoyed admiring Bell's gift when no one else was about, something she couldn't admit to Bell for fear of confusing the little girl.

"Do you think Abby will like it?"

Lily blinked, drawn out of her thoughts to admire the fine work Bell had done.

The small linen cloth had flowers sewn along its border, each yellow petal filled in with even, straight stitches. The crowning decoration had to be Abigail's nickname rather than her initials set out so finely it seemed as though Bell had used a quill rather than needle and thread.

"I think she will love it. You put my own work to shame." Lily twisted to share this amazing skill with her lady's maid as she'd never been able to share Sam's talents, but her gaze fell on the empty chair that should have held Kate.

Bell put a hand on Lily's knee. "I'm sorry I can't be more like her. I'm sorry having me here makes you sad."

Lily twisted to face the girl, aware shock showed in her widened eyes and rounded mouth.

She shook her head quickly, realizing Bell meant her sister not Kate. "Whatever makes you say such a thing? Having you here makes me happier than I've been since Sam left. And while you're nothing like my sister, neither are you meant to be a replacement. I see you as you are, not some shadow of Sam. She'll always be in my thoughts and heart, but there's room enough for you as well."

Bell stared at the floor, one foot twisting against the carpet laid there, but at last, she peeked up through loose black locks.

"Do you really mean that?"

Lily tossed her embroidery aside and pulled Bell into a hug. "Of course I mean that. You have no idea how lonely I was before you came. I mean, the staff has their duties, Henry is off in London, and with Kate gone…"

"That's your lady's maid, isn't it? I hear the others talking about her sometimes."

An unexpected laugh burst from Lily as she ruffled the top of Bell's hair. "In that one aspect, you and my sister are like twins. I was ever telling her not to listen to the household gossip, but still she would plague me with questions founded not in truth but in rumors overheard or told straight to her."

A blush tinged Bell's pale cheeks, but still she said, "They don't seem to like her much."

Lily wondered just what the girl had overheard. Could she have learned how Kate felt toward those with a Natural's gifts?

"They're just happy without Kate to keep them in strict order. Henry's housekeeper stayed on in the London town house so the place could be set to rights whenever he and I came up. Kate took on many of the housekeeper's duties when we arrived, and the others must resent her orders to some degree."

Bell watched her steadily for a long moment then nodded. "Our cook never did like the head maid either."

Though she said nothing more as she returned to her seat and chose a second square of linen, Lily kept an eye on the girl, wondering if she would reveal another piece of her life before arriving at the manor doorstep. When Bell concentrated on her work instead, Lily's thoughts returned to the absent Kate.

The household staff might feel her time away to be a holiday, but Lily missed sharing humorous moments with her lady's maid, and there had been plenty since Bell joined their family.

She hadn't wanted to admit it at first, but she should never have let Henry send Kate off like that. Such a harsh reaction seemed unreasonable now when all Kate had said was what everyone else might have thought, rightly or wrongly. As much as they could wish the lady's maid had opened her heart to Sam, they could hardly condemn her for believing what all the world did.

It spoke to their close relationship that the woman felt able to speak her mind, and yet how had Lily reacted? The statement deserved a strong scolding for sure, but nothing more than that. Instead, Henry had supported Lily as he always did. He'd sent Kate off to her father's cottage where Lily wouldn't have to see her and be reminded of her condemnation of Sam, or perhaps simply the reminder of Sam's unknown state.

She wondered what Kate had found to occupy herself. Did she sit in the small home where she'd grown up and think on what Lily used to keep busy?

The questions brought forth a spike of guilt as she realized after Abigail had been too flustered to remember the first night, she'd failed to take the medicinal tea Kate always prepared for her. With summer coming and her feeling so much stronger, there hadn't seemed the need, but she knew Kate would not be happy to learn she'd neglected her health.

Lily's gaze found Bell once again. Kate would have more to face than a few missed teas.

Would the lady's maid welcome the child in their midst? Surely word had spread through the village about the foundling. Kate's father would have brought back the tale from the local tavern even if Kate kept to the cottage and her father's garden.

Bell's attention remained fixed, proof of how she managed such beautiful work when even Lily became distracted.

Kate would find much to love in this child when she'd thought Sam little better than a ruffian. Together they could continue Bell's schooling in the finer marks of behavior until the little girl would do them proud even in London itself.

Lily remembered her talk with Henry, the vision of a younger Sam hiding in her skirts replaced with Bell and sitting less awkwardly. Somehow, she doubted Bell would have as much trouble resisting the call of anything mechanical. She had only to look at how well the child had done here. With the exception of a few glances in the direction of the workshop, Bell had shown little sign of her nature.

The realization only made Lily miss her little sister more. Sam might never have been the best behaved, but she'd had a smile for everyone in her path and found joy where another would only sadness. A wave of that emotion crashed over Lily and threatened what little peace she'd managed. She turned her thoughts back to Kate when she could do nothing to improve her sister's circumstances.

Despite Kate's failings on the subject of Naturals, she'd always been kind and loyal. She would have to see how good Bell had been for Lily and welcome the girl. Perhaps Bell's more ladylike behavior would win the maid over where Sam never had. Perhaps she could even turn Kate away from what all of England held to be true regarding Naturals, though only if Bell's knack stayed hidden long enough to secure Kate's affection.

Lily decided she would welcome Kate's return instead of dread the risks the lady's maid represented. With Henry gone, Lily had no one to share her delight in Bell with, or to discuss what planning they should be about for the household either. There could be no doubt Bell had won over every other person in the household. Why would Kate prove any different?

*H*ENRY HAD WRITTEN TO THOSE hoping for a meeting as soon as he'd arrived back in London, but still the acceptances pouring in for the dinner he'd suggested amazed him. With such short notice, a bare five days, surely most of them had engagements already.

He laughed as Bessie handed him another letter, her entrance into the study escaping his notice until then.

Perhaps he'd found the true answer for the eagerness after all. Important business for Parliament would surely hold precedence over some dinner party or even a ball these men had been pressed into attending.

Had he any female relatives, he'd most likely think the same, though should Lily feel well enough to come to London, he'd happily escort her to whatever might catch her fancy.

"That had better be the last of your guests or the roast won't be enough to serve them."

Even Bessie's scowl couldn't dent his enthusiasm. "Perhaps you should send for another one if the pantry has gone lacking."

She threw both hands in the air, startling him. "As if it could be so easy. That meat's been in the oven these two hours past. Takes more than a quick run to the butcher to put down a feast for fourteen or more."

Henry stared at his housekeeper, taking in her white cap that sat slightly askew and the frown lines cutting into her forehead.

"It's not too much for you, is it?" he asked in a belated realization more than the members' schedules had been disrupted.

She heaved a deep sigh then shook her head. "I'm not the one cooking it. Still, while this might not be as fancy as they've come to expect in some of the London houses, they won't go wanting. We've made sure of that much."

Henry gave her arm a light squeeze. "I do not know what I'd do without you."

A sparkle lit her eye, and she said only, "Starve," as she spun on her heel and headed back into the servant area, presumably to check on the state of the dinner.

Henry wondered what Bessie would think of his latest approach. Would she see it as a form of the slavery that had swept up so many from her native home? Or would she see it as an opportunity for Naturals to work hard and earn the respect of other Englishmen as she had?

The thought kept him occupied until time to dress before the first of his guests arrived. It was not enough to prove Naturals had economic value. He had to figure out how they were to keep the freedom he sought for them by bartering their talents.

Henry arrived downstairs just as Bessie answered the door. He had seen no need for a butler when he never entertained at home. Now he wondered whether he asked too much of Bessie, especially after the condescension offered her by the clerk the other day.

"The guests are gathering in the front parlor. Follow me if you please."

He needn't have worried. Rather than chance a repeat, Bessie had adopted an attitude every bit as lofty as the strictest butler he'd had the misfortune to encounter.

Smothering a laugh, Henry ducked into the servant's section and used a back way he'd taken advantage of often enough to get ahead of his brother when they were boys. The maid he encountered, after a yelp of surprise, promised to pass on a request for tea as he raced by. Though he planned for wine with dinner and sherry afterward, he wanted his guests as clearheaded for their discussions as possible.

He was already ensconced in a high-backed armchair when Bessie led Lord Bartford through the door, though it had been close. Bessie swallowed her surprise like an expert as she gave a quick curtsy and returned to her post.

Henry rose to return a bow in greeting. "My staff will bring tea shortly."

Lord Bartford coughed in what could only be an attempt to mask a chuckle. "Intending to keep us sharp?" the older man said.

There seemed no value in pretending otherwise, so Henry inclined his head and waved Lord Bartford to a chair.

"We have much to discuss. It seemed only wise."

Lord Bartford leaned forward to brace his arms on his knees. "You are aware that most will come out of curiosity. It's not often such radical thought rises from the older titles."

"Do you consider yourself part of that group, Lord Bartford? It's my understanding you bought your title with hard work and good management. I would have thought you one of those better able to see the truth in my statements." Henry kept his tone light, careful not to offend, but wanting to establish his choice in this particular group of men from the start.

This time, Lord Bartford did laugh aloud. "I've heard some fascinating stories about the Stapletons. It seems the tales might have held as much fact as fiction. Quite an unusual lord you are."

Henry smiled. "I will take that as a compliment, though I do not know which stories you refer to. It could as easily be a curse."

Lord Bartford slapped his thigh and laughed again. "Yes, yes, a compliment, my boy. Your ideas might be against what is known, but your heart's in the right place."

Letting the familiarity pass without protest, Henry met a gaze holding more knowing awareness than he'd anticipated.

If Lord Bartford suspected what drove Henry to seek economic motivations to achieve the aims he'd raised in his first speech, at least the man did not appear to scorn him for it. The lord's presence here suggested he'd be willing to offer support for the second, but perhaps this statement meant as much support would be found for the need to ensure the freedom of those Naturals brought to industry.

The other guests began arriving in clusters, which, along with the tea, prevented further exploration for the moment, but Henry secreted the knowledge away for later perusal. Cultivating advocates could only improve his chances, and that of the Naturals who had been mistreated by the law.

For now, though, custom dictated the discussion turn more to general topics, allowing Henry a peek into the London season with the perspectives of both the old guard and new. He noted the predominance of younger men and thought on Lord Bartford as he wondered if he'd been misguided in choosing to focus on the young. This dinner seemed likely to provide as much food for thought as it filled his stomach, and all that before they retired to discuss the business at hand.

18

Dinner would be called at any moment, and none too soon if the faint rumbles from Bell's stomach were any measure. Lily heard a sound at the door and turned to tell Abigail they'd be right in.

Kate stood in the doorway, her eyes filled with worry for her mistress and her body bound by a hesitation that sat oddly on the lady's maid.

Lily smiled and raised both hands to draw her within. "Oh, Kate, I am glad to see you here."

The lady's maid started, then crossed the room to accept Lily's welcome. "I'm happy to be back," she said, clearly eager to dismiss their past argument as Lily had done.

Bell shifted in her position on the floor, turning to face them both.

Lily could tell when Kate noticed the movement because her hands tensed before falling away.

"She's ba—" Kate's words choked off at the sight of Bell, dark hair held tidily in a ribbon, wearing a nice dress, and with shoes on her little feet.

"Kate, this is Bell. She's an orphan who has come to live with us."

All worries vanished as Kate flashed a grin at Lily before examining Bell more thoroughly.

"Oh, mistress, you have such a generous heart. And what a beautiful little girl you've rescued. There's so many in those foundling houses as deserve so much more. You and the lord will make wonderful parents. You deserve children, that you do. Good children. This is the perfect solution."

Some of Kate's tension transferred to Lily's shoulders at the hint of her childless state, but Lily took a deep breath and let it pass. She focused instead on how Kate welcomed Bell.

"You look to have some skills, Bell, isn't it?" Kate had crouched next to the little girl and was admiring her tight stitches.

If not for choosing the floor when she found the chairs too tall, Bell could have been any wealthy child. Cook had made a mission of plumping away all signs of the girl's time of scavenging, and Lily had worked hard with Bell to sew Sam's old clothes to fit rather than just rolling them up at the waist. The extra cloth now lay hidden in tidy seams for when the girl grew.

Abigail arrived at the door then to call them to dinner.

"I'll be about unpacking my things," Kate said, brushing her skirt as she rose.

Just when Lily thought that to be the end of it, though, Kate paused.

"I am sorry," she said in an unusually soft tone. "I regret my hasty words before. I needed to use my brain not my tongue and will strive to do better in the future."

The delighted welcome Kate gave Bell left Lily in too good a mood to hold on to what had happened even had she wanted to.

"It's forgotten," Lily said in as soft a voice. "It is good to have you home."

Kate smiled and nodded. "And for things to be back to normal, I'd guess. I can't imagine Abby's proven much help."

Lily bit down a protest when she had to admit, while Abigail proved pleasant company, her skills had been as lacking as her ability to focus on one task at a time.

"Normal has changed." She indicated Bell with her chin. "But some return will be welcome."

"I'll have everything made ready for you to rest after dinner. I'll start your tea brewing now."

Kate didn't stay for another word, but the mention of the nasty tea had been enough. Lily fought down the urge to stick out her tongue at the retreating back, a bad habit she'd picked up from Bell despite the girl's otherwise polite nature.

"She seems nice enough," the girl said, climbing to her feet now that Kate had left.

Lily rose as well, reaching out to tug a strand of Bell's black hair in thanks for the reminder. "She is. She just has some traditional thoughts is all."

Any ungratefulness about the bitter tea's return, or the assumption she still retired early even for country hours, were undeserved. The woman had only Lily's good health in mind and had not been here to see how well Lily had been doing. It would take some adjustments as they found a new routine, but having everyone where they belonged could be nothing but good.

As Bell skipped ahead to the dining room, to all appearances a normal girl, Lily's thoughts veered to the one truth they could not reveal. Kate might be happy Lily and Henry found a child to dote on now, but her reaction to Sam left little doubt as to what she'd think of Bell's nature should it be revealed.

Lily brushed that worry aside. Bell had shown no difficulty in hiding her talents. Why would that change now just because the need to remain concealed had grown all the stronger?

*T*HE LIVELY DINNER PROVED THIS group of men had strong feelings and conviction on a variety of topics. Whether new to their responsibilities or having warmed a seat in Parliament for some time, they'd showed themselves to be thinking men.

"Shall we retire to the parlor, gentlemen?" Henry asked as he pushed back his chair.

Their numbers were too large for his study, but with no wife in residence, the parlor remained unoccupied. They'd be more comfortable there, and Henry wanted them at ease.

Upon entering, Henry strode across the carpet to the far end of the room where Bessie had set out a decanter and small glasses. The gentlemen could find chairs where they would, and he wanted to get to the heart of this engagement promptly. As much as he'd enjoyed the conversations before, a part of him rang with the need to get things moving. After all, Bell now stood at risk as much as Sam.

"So have you any proof of what you claim?" One of the younger lords, Lord Jackfeld, said into the silence that had fall-en.

Henry jerked, almost spilling brandy from the glass in his hand. He turned to face the others, meeting the gaze of Lord Jackfeld then scanning the rest. Only curiosity met his questing.

"I have never seen a Natural at work like a blacksmith if that's your meaning," he replied in a mild tone, staying as close to the truth as he could. "But I have seen the results of their labors all too near me. Had my life and that of my team not been at risk when we faced the Natural, the sheer creativity and complexity of the mechanisms set against us would have been impressive."

Under their questioning, Henry realized he'd noticed more than he'd thought in that one encounter when he'd been an officer. He wondered how much of his reaction to learning the truth about Sam had been influenced by his admiration of the Natural's skills rather than his guilt in the face of the man's desperation.

Henry fought the urge to slip some of Sam's work into the mix, knowing he could not afford to attract any attention even now. Still, it seemed he'd caught their interest.

Lord Bartford stood, bringing the conversation to a sudden halt. "How do we know these skills can be put to uses other than violence? While The Queen's army might rejoice in mechanical soldiers, I certainly wouldn't want to purchase a turning spit that might someday stab my kitchen staff."

Henry gave the man a sharp look, having expected an advocate of the supportive sort, not one to cut through any positive thinking.

"I'm not denying there is purpose to this direction of inquiry," Lord Bartford said in answer to the look. "I mean only that we need to consider the dangers as well. You might want to think confining Naturals came about because of ownership concerns, but there are as many reports of injuries as any loss of property."

Henry thrust a hand through his hair before pushing upright as well. "Does a fox bite when cornered?"

"We've heard this argument already," Lord Bartford protested.

Henry nodded an acknowledgement but persisted in his point regardless. "The analogy is apt if you'd but think on it. Why do we hunt foxes?"

He didn't wait for someone else to answer the question. "Because they steal chickens, not because they are dangerous. And yet, there are many who have been harmed or seen harm to their dogs because of the hunt."

With a shrug, Lord Bartford sank to his seat once again, conceding the point.

Henry did not copy the move. Instead, he began to pace, his thoughts spinning wildly.

"I still have friends among those on the police force. They told me a story that speaks even stronger for changing these laws. They told me of a man—a good, hardworking Englishman like any of us—captured and almost confined to an asylum for the rest of his life based on malicious rumors started to punish him for some slight.

"This tells me two things. The first is simply anyone around us could be a Natural. There are no outward signs of either madness or talent until they feel threatened. The second is where the laws make no sense. There are those who would use them for foul means, making the police into a private enforcement team not for the good of society but for one man's vendettas."

Mr. Maxwell shook his head, laughing. "Save your speechifying for the floor, Lord Stapleton. You've already won us over by the possibilities or we wouldn't be here. No need to scare us with the consequences."

The others joined in with the laughter at that, and Henry felt his cheeks heat.

"I apologize. It's only that I spend my time trying to figure out ways to make this right, and thinking on all the ways it can be so wrong."

Mr. Maxwell accepted his apology with a quick nod before seizing the key elements of Henry's point. "If the only Naturals we know of are those gone into berserker rages, how are we to find a Natural willing to work with us to prove this possibility sound?"

Henry went to reply, but one of the other young lords cut in first.

"There've been rumors of a Natural around my country estate. Just some odd events that didn't quite add up, but which could easily have a Natural at the root, especially considering how Lord Stapleton pointed out they could be any of us."

That last sent many a gaze skittering around the room only to end in a shared, if awkward, laugh.

"Even here, gathered as we are to improve the lot of Naturals," Henry said, "you have only to think on your own reactions to recognize the example you're looking for can't be found. Not here. What Natural would come forward, even under our protections, knowing they could never return to safety in obscurity even if the laws were changed? It will take much more than wiping out an unjust law to relieve a fear that has been cultivated for so long."

That brought forth some grumbles and consternation, but better they understood what lay ahead.

"So we are to move forward, to stand our word behind yours, based on nothing more than supposition?" an older gentleman put forth.

Henry shrugged, feigning a casual state. "Were the original Natural laws put into place with any more evidence? Naturals weren't hunted then. It's been long enough most don't remember, but there was a time when Naturals lived alongside every other Englishman and woman without drawing any specific attention."

Slowly, his words sunk in, and he received accepting nods in return, unsurprising considering as how these gentlemen came here because they were already open to the argument.

Henry pushed aside his own thoughts of why the Naturals became visible now, so visible they provoked the Natural laws. They'd clearly been among the people for a long time, even before their gifts manifested. Just because the objects triggering bouts had yet to come into being was no reason to suppose the knack hadn't been present.

In the short time he'd contemplated what he'd left out of his telling, the others had broken into smaller groups to discuss their approaches. Henry drifted from group to group, adding the occasional comment but largely listening.

He'd been hoping to gain strong advocates who would be willing to stand up and speak with him. In these, he found that hope, but they were the thinking men he'd believed them to be. As such, they were not willing to take only his word for it.

"What if we brought someone to speak to Parliament who has had firsthand experience," one of the young gentlemen asked.

"Lord Stapleton has already spoken."

"No, he's right," Lord Bartford said. "Not a member of Parliament, but another authority."

"I know just the man. He's part of the police force," Henry interjected into the conversation. "They're probably the only ones to have first-hand experience and be willing to talk about it."

The others didn't take long to agree, drawing in the full number as they planned how to make this occur.

Henry allowed himself a slight smile at their enthusiasm and commitment. Everything he'd hoped for and yet held little expectation of achieving. With so many voices where first there had been only one, surely Parliament would stand firm against him no longer.

19

Kate was surprised to hear Lily's plans the next morning, but soon the lady's maid looked forward to their gambols across the manor grounds. Lily laughed aloud to see the ribbon Kate had secured around Sunshine's neck so he could walk beside them. While Bell kept close at hand until released to gather flowers, Sunshine reminded Lily of Sam's delight in a large world she could safely enjoy. Like with any limits she'd put on Sam, the kitten pulled at the end of the rope from the very start, eager to explore. One of the stable boys had come up with a harness to keep the kitten in check or he would have escaped the ribbon that first day.

Lily released her worries about Bell winning Kate over as she watched the little girl instruct Kate in the best way to create a flower crown though the lady's maid had probably been making her own since before Bell was born. Apparently, Kate's efforts the previous day had been less than satisfactory.

The joy this little girl brought them balanced out any concerns, and her control continued to amaze Lily.

Lily and Henry had grown so solemn even before Sam left, a state only apparent now with smiles and laughter echoing around the manor. If her sister had been able to keep her knack quiet as Bell could, they would never have had to send her away in the first place, but then if she had done so, she wouldn't have been Sam at all.

Lily stumbled on the path, but straightened before the others noticed. Whatever strength Sunshine, Bell, and the approaching summer had brought no longer held firm. Each day, she felt a little weaker. Soon, Lily would not be able to go with them into the fields. She'd be stuck in the sitting room with a fire, her hands too shaky even to do needlework. At least she had good memories to dwell on, and recent laughter to raise her spirits. It had become all too easy to set her sights on the end. She'd forgotten to treasure each day until the time came as if it were her last.

"We'd best be heading back," Kate said, appearing at Lily's side unnoticed. "I have chores to do, and I'm sure there are activities you've been neglecting as well what with all these picnics you've been on. We can find something inside to occupy the young miss."

Not wanting to dampen the joy Kate and Bell shared, Lily had been hiding her growing weakness, but she had no strength to protest and gratefully accepted the better excuse. They waited for Bell to skip over with Sunshine, and Lily laced her arm through Kate's as if to share in the delight rather than needing the support.

Kate, though, had not been fooled judging by the frown she shot in Lily's direction. "I'm thinking you'll be off to bed early tonight, mistress. We wouldn't want you sickening again."

As much as Lily wanted to pretend it wasn't so, by the time the sky had grown dark that night, she welcomed the comfort of her mattress.

"Now drink your tea and lay down your head."

Kate lifted the cup toward Lily, and she took it, though she'd rather have completed the second command alone and gone right to sleep. The tea made her nose wrinkle and her throat tighten as it always did, but if it had any chance of helping, she'd suffer the bitter taste and more only to have a little longer to spend with Henry and Bell.

Bell climbed in next to Lily and wrapped both arms around her, seeming much younger than she normally did with this clear sign of Lily's frailty. The little girl had lost so much already. It seemed cruel to bind her close when Lily would soon be gone as well.

Kate shook her head. "When the master returns, you'll be off to your own room for sure," she scolded Bell, but the smile on her face proved she'd fallen as much under the spell the little girl cast as any of them.

Nor did she pull Bell from the bed. At least the little girl would have others who cared for her when the time came. As long as she kept the secret, at least.

"Thank you, Kate," Lily murmured, her eyes already slipping closed. With the warmth of Bell snug against her, she let exhaustion win.

Kate had returned just in time. While the girl had proved quite the restorative for a while, with the added responsibility for Bell, Lily needed all the assistance she could obtain. Nothing seemed to have a lasting positive effect on her health.

Bell's cuddles were no different than Kate's teas or Henry's attempts to change the Natural laws. They all sensed the truth and needed to do something, no matter how futile, so they did not stew in the reality of her decline. One short period of improvement aside, what ailed Lily had more strength than even a kitten or precious child could counter.

A sharp longing for her own mother pierced Lily. She wanted to return to her childhood where a soft word and the brush of a hand to her forehead could make everything all right. She had more in common with Bell than the little girl would ever know, and just as Sam had vanished from Lily's life, Bell would suffer that tearing pain when Lily left the manor without even the slender hope of her coming to visit as Sam had been given. Another false promise.

*H*ENRY SENT THE REQUEST FOR a formal meeting with Parson to the station the very next day. Asking a man to give evidence seemed a little more than something he could just drop into casual conversation. Still, he hadn't expected the inspector to want a piece of the discussion when he'd arrived at the arranged time some three days later.

"And that's the full of it. I have many in both Houses willing to address this wrong, but they want to hear from someone other than myself. They also think to sway even more with the testimony of a respected member of the police force."

He stopped talking, his gaze not on Parson but on the inspector's face. The man had aged a good bit in the time Henry had been absent, but neither the strength nor intelligence in his piercing stare had weakened.

"I should have known it would be you come back to stir up trouble, Lord Stapleton. If you weren't the type, you'd never have crossed the doorstep out yonder so many years ago."

Henry said nothing, hoping his restraint would sway this man to his side.

"Parson will be called upon only to give an account of his experiences? No tricking one of my officers into untruths with the weight of your history?"

Suppressing a grimace, Henry shook his head. "I want only a true accounting, though he may be asked to speak on his own reactions."

The inspector glanced from one to the other of them and gave a slight smile. "This is where you will rest your case, if I'm not mistaken. I suspect you two are of one mind on the issue."

Parson started, but the inspector waved him to silence.

"You think you're the only one who is uncomfortable with the direction things have been going, Parson? I've seen more change in my lifetime than any man should, and some of it is downright unpleasant. I might not be ready to charge forth and stick my neck out for those who, like as not, come to my attention only because they've broken one law or another, but Lord Stapleton makes a good argument. If you trap a starving rat, should you be surprised when he chews his way out through your hand?"

The man gave a decisive nod and pushed to his feet in clear dismissal. "I'll leave the choice to your conscience, Parson, though I suspect your mind is already made up."

He leveled his stare on Henry. "I won't have my station become a place of politicking though. These are unusual circumstances for an unusual law. There aren't many who have experience with Naturals beyond the officers, and if they do, they certainly won't be coming forward in support of the idea."

Henry opened his mouth to protest but was cut off when the inspector raised a hand.

"I meant only to say those with other experiences risk deportation or imprisonment for aiding a fugitive. It's a situation that sits poorly with me. Just as all Naturals are made criminal for their nature, all those around them are given the choice between the pan and the fire."

At that, his smile broadened. "You have the passion of your father, Lord Stapleton. You do him proud. Now get yourselves out of my office. I have proper business to attend to."

Henry followed Parson out, feeling dazed.

All this time, he'd had no idea the inspector knew his father personally, but from the comment, they'd clearly belonged to the same circles. A chuckle slipped out at the thought. Suddenly his acceptance into the rank and file seemed a little too easy for a lord's second son. If any others among the nobility had wanted such a position, they would have been given an inspector's rank or quietly steered in the other direction.

"I always knew he had a liking for you, Henry. Wouldn't have been so sharp otherwise."

Henry shook his head. "I certainly never suspected."

Parson rubbed his chin and said, "I'd guess you're looking at those years on the streets a little differently now. But before you start to doubt, let me remind you how the people felt. You were a good officer. If some rubbing elbows gave you the chance, you certainly earned the right to be there once you were."

Shaking off the question, Henry caught Parson by the shoulder. "You will speak, won't you?"

"Do you have to ask? There are enough out on the streets intending to do harm. I see neither the reason to create others nor the need to waste more resources better spent on true criminals. I'll speak to your Parliament, and I'll stand by you in this. You had only to ask."

When Parson split off to rejoin his team, Henry wandered in the direction of his home, wondering just how he'd tell Lily of this latest development. A wave of homesickness, not for the manor but for his lovely wife, crashed over him. He wanted so much to be there with her. To tell her in person what a letter could not safely convey for sure, but as much because she'd been doing so well, better perhaps than he'd seen her for years.

Still, he had only to think on what progress he'd made to know his time in London had not been wasted.

Henry came here for Lily's sake, for Sam, for Bell, and for all those burdened with the Natural laws. With Parson to testify on behalf of the Naturals, to speak plainly about what environment such unjust laws create, the members would have to listen. They'd have to give full consideration, knowing it would take little to turn such laws against other groups, and little to see themselves on the wrong side of it.

If he could bring a controlled Natural before them, they'd have to question their own eyes, but such could not be accomplished safely until after the laws were changed, or at least under reconsideration. He would not put any person at risk in that fashion.

Bell seemed so young to hold onto silence, and he didn't know if she would remember to hide when asked about her abilities, but Sam had been even younger when Lily first became responsible for her. Lily knew exactly how to keep a young Natural occupied and safe when confined to the manor and the grounds. As loyal as his household proved to be time and again, even with their fears, both Lily and Bell would be safe there until he could ensure their safety for all time.

His legs stretched of their own accord, lengthening his stride and shortening the distance to home and the letter sure to be waiting for him.

Lily had written every day since he last left, and each time she managed to find some way to soothe his fears about Bell's reticence.

He treasured each word, able to hear Lily's voice behind them in how the sentences were put together. And Bell seemed every bit the delightful child he'd met. Even Kate, now returned from her father's cottage, was by all accounts captivated.

Remembering how having small tinkers to work on had helped Sam, Henry vowed to purchase some mechanical toys to bring back with him. As long as Bell took care not to change them too much, she could use such to prevent her Natural energy from bottling up and coming forth all in a rush as had happened to Sam when first they'd tried to keep her from working on anything at all.

Isolation, restriction, and imprisonment.

None were happy or fair ways to treat those special few with such a knack. As much as he longed to be at Lily's side, his purpose was to be found in London. He refused to let down all the faceless Naturals any more than he would the two who had joined his life.

Somehow, he suspected it might be harder to persuade the populace than Parliament if Naturals were to come free from every nook and cranny once their status improved. Like as not, though, while they might be wary of strangers, most would know at least one person who had been hiding such skills. Perhaps a friend or relative living among them in secrecy, or even a lover or parent. As the inspector said, the law punished more than just those with the knack, whether the others complied or fought its rulings.

One simple change, and England would be a better place for all her people.

20

Lily woke to find Bell still curled beside her. As much as she wanted to nudge the little girl awake and set off on another adventure, she found her hand shaking when she raised it off the blanket. By the time Kate came to open the drapes, Lily still hadn't gathered the energy to rise.

"I'm thinking a quiet day in the parlor will do you a world of good, mistress," Kate announced in a calm tone, her face still turned toward the window.

Lily sighed inwardly, knowing the look of concern Kate hid all too well.

"That sounds lovely," she replied with an equally false cheer. She knew better than to hope, or should have.

Bell sat up and rubbed her eyes, blinking in the light.

A chuckle teased its way out of Kate, and Lily joined her, the sight so much like when Sunshine stretched and yawned his way out of a nap.

Lily brushed a hand over Bell's head. No matter how weak she might feel, having Bell in their lives had brought more joy than Lily had ever thought she would experience once Sam left them. Though the many outings most likely contributed to her current decline, she did not regret a moment of them.

"What are we doing today?"

The innocent question soured Lily's enjoyment, but she forced a smile as she said, "There's mending to be done, my dear. We can't always be playing, you know."

Where Lily had expected a protest, Bell only tossed back the covers and slid off the bed. She glanced to Lily as though waiting for her to do the same.

Laughing once more, Lily copied her charge, though she moved not to the door but the basin of wash water.

"We have to get clean and dressed first, Bell. Your eagerness is grand, but I'm too hungry to labor on an empty stomach."

Despite her weakness and being trapped inside, the rest of the day followed much the same. If Lily grew melancholy, she had only to look to Bell to find some joy once again. Henry's absence, though, weighed all the heavier with her confined and idle. At least when they had been roaming the estate, she'd been busy enough to be distracted.

Lily glanced at the sitting room clock for what must be the third time in the hour. Today had no more reason to herald Henry's return than any other, but time seemed to have slowed to a crawl.

She looked again, frowning. Time had not slowed, it had stopped altogether.

The mantle clock seemed to mock her wish for Henry as though her life had stood still since he'd left for London. Worse, she'd denied Sam the clock to play with more times than she could remember only to have it fail on her now.

She laughed at herself, drawing a quick look from Bell before the girl returned to her games.

Most likely the clock required no more than winding, a task Henry enjoyed performing almost as much as his mechanical man enjoyed helping as the pocket watch opened the glass over its face to show Henry the exact time. Which brought her back to Henry's absence with a sigh.

Bell glanced up from where she played with a rag doll one of the servants had found for her, but Lily only shook her head and the girl returned to her silent game. What ailed her was not something even a talented Natural could fix.

The open door revealed no sign of the servants or anyone who could help her.

She looked at Bell once again. This Natural had more control than Sam ever had. Bell never gave the clock any attention, at least that Lily had observed. She showed none of the craving it provoked in Lily's sister.

"Bell, could you reach down the mantle clock and bring it to me to wind?"

The clock would be better if not moved, but she could not bear to have time frozen any more than she could rise to wind it where the clock belonged. Kate would have to set it later. Even unset, though, the hands would march around its face, bringing Henry's return ever closer.

Bell placed the doll on the table and crossed to get the clock down.

Lily watched her closely but could see no indication she wanted the clock for any purpose other than to bring it to the couch as requested. There were times like these when she was hard pressed to think of Bell as a Natural.

From the little Bell had said of her parents, Lily suspected her control came at least in part from having grown up sheltered and loved. Sam had all the love they could spare her, but every moment had been tainted with the knowledge that she had to stay hidden, that no one else could even know she lived at all.

"Now fetch me the key," Lily said once the clock lay in her hands. If they'd been out in the country from the start, maybe

Sam would have known such comfort instead of the fear she'd been raised on from much too young an age.

Now Lily tore the same from Bell, telling her to hide her nature and lie about what she was in truth.

As Lily wound, though, she realized Sam would have been no safer if she'd still been here at the manor.

Bell came to them not as a confident, loved little girl but the very fugitive they'd feared Sam would become. Her parents clearly loved her and would only have sent her running across the fields if they had no choice. Any safety the countryside offered was as much illusion as truth. It would take a single misspoken word, not even a malicious act, and Bell would be on the run again…if she weren't caught immediately. This had been what drove Henry to London in the first place after all.

Lily stared down at the clock, her mind confident in the decision to send her sister away while her heart clung to the dream of safety here at home. All this would have been so much easier if only they knew Sam had made her way to the safe haven and wasn't in any danger.

"It's still not ticking," Bell said, her head tipped to one side as she tried to hear the sound. "When Father wound our clocks, they started right up…or never stopped at all."

Though her gaze had snapped to the little girl, now Lily looked back at the clock in her lap though her ears told the same story as Bell had.

"It must be damaged somehow, or worn out. Henry will be so disappointed."

"I could try to fix it."

Remembering the small toy Bell had made her, and still driven by the fear she'd broken her sister in the name of pro-tection, Lily handed the mantel clock over.

"Just to fix it," she murmured.

Bell hefted the solid wood and set it down on the table for her workspace. "I know you want it the same. I'll only look for what is broken."

Lily stared at the little girl, stunned at how easily she dismissed the call of a mechanical.

Sometimes, when Sam said a mechanical had a weak draw, her sister had been able to describe what the mechanism longed to be. But never without visible effort.

Lily missed those moments when she could share in some aspect of Sam's gift, but they came rarely, and she knew how much they'd cost her sister as Sam fought for control.

Though Bell clearly heard Sam's creations just as she must have felt something from the clock Sam had studiously ignored whenever in this room, maybe Bell had a weaker gift. Perhaps that, not any trick of her upbringing, gave her the control Sam had always longed for.

A knife appeared from somewhere, though Lily had not seen it about before, and Bell carefully unscrewed the back to get at the works. The tools might be like Sam, but this effort showed none of the preternatural speed Sam used when in a bout. Bell moved with the slow intensity of a clockmaker. Lily wondered what this girl could offer the world. Unlike when desperation drove Sam to repair or transform, Bell had both skill and control.

ENRY RECEIVED WORD PARLIAMENT WOULD hear Parson's testimony four days hence as he sat down to a lonely breakfast. The missive sent him to his desk without even finishing his cup of tea despite the scolding he could expect from Bessie. He had only secured Parson's agreement the day before. One of his new friends must have influenced the schedule.

As he marshaled the words to convey this promising news to Lily, Henry skimmed her previous letters. They allowed him to be close to her in the only way available. But when it came time to put pen to paper, the same instincts that served him well at Parson's side told him something was not quite right.

He reread the letters more slowly this time, taking care to consider each word, and the pattern he'd noticed subconsciously sprang clear from the page.

Henry surged to his feet, calling out to Bessie to send for his horse. He'd tell Lily the news first hand and see for himself how she fared. The hope Kate's return had offered seemed false now with each letter speaking of outings closer to the house even without the waver in Lily's fine handwriting. He'd dismissed it as excitement before, but no longer.

His urgency faded not one bit as he rode out of London as fast as the horse could carry him, stopping only once for a quick meal. He had no intention of arriving at his wife's side starving and half wild. Not when he knew her first thought would be to the little girl who had captured Lily's heart. Neither would he waste an extra minute.

Part of him feared even now he'd be too late. She'd have gone beyond his grasp for good, and his loneliness would never end.

Henry shoved that thought away, determination keeping him steady when nothing else remained.

He hoped he'd discover upon his arrival that fear, not instinct, drove him. That he'd find Lily as strong if not stronger than she'd been when last he had seen her.

She had to be.

21

Bell's methodical workings lulled Lily into a doze, her head sinking further into the cushions on the couch where she lay resting. Every once in a while, a ticking would start up or the chime would sound, but so far, despite working for hours, Bell had failed to restore the clock.

A shocked gasp came from the door and pulled Lily into full awareness. Before she could react, Kate marched through the door and grabbed Bell's arm.

"You naughty little slip of a girl," Kate charged. "Why, that clock has been in this family longer than you've been alive. The mistress loves it as much as the master ever did and here you are dismantling it as though we haven't given you toys a plenty."

"Kate, don't."

Lily realized her lady's maid must have been unaware of her presence until that moment, but her intercession came too late.

Kate stumbled, recognizing the look that came over Bell's face as much as Lily had.

Where before the girl worked slowly, now her movements grew blurred and held a frantic air as she tackled the broken mantle clock with more than her normal skills. Bell proved as susceptible to panic as ever Sam had been.

Kate turned to Lily, betrayal mixed into the shock in her gaze. "You knew. You brought her here, brought another monster into our lives, and you knew. This is not some orphan you adopted out of the goodness of your heart. It's a Natural most likely drawn by that workshop where you keep all the machines your sister made instead of destroying them for the good of everyone."

She practically spat the last, and Lily fought her own temper as she put out a hand to calm the maid. The anger was deserved at least in part as she had deceived them all. Lily had hoped to reveal the truth about Bell in a softer fashion, especially to Kate.

She lowered her arm when Kate shifted away rather than accept the touch.

"Bell is no different now than she was yesterday when she went skipping at your side. Or this morning, when you laughed at her sleepy expression. She's just a little girl."

Kate scowled, glancing between Lily and Bell. "She's not just anything, especially not a little girl. She's the devil himself in a kind skin so we won't see it coming. Who knows what she's doing to the clock, or what it will do to us once she's done."

Fear swept Kate's features but it kept her from attempting to snatch the clock from Bell, a choice that made Lily grateful.

She'd never seen Bell in a full bout, but knew well enough what fear could drive a Natural to do. There had been that knife somewhere around here.

Kate fell to her knees beside the couch and caught Lily's hands in her own.

"Surely you can see the danger, mistress. Send her away. There's waifs enough who would delight in making this their home, ones who wouldn't turn around and change the very floor beneath your feet. Turn her in to those who know how to contain one of her kind."

Lily jerked her hands free and glared at the lady's maid. "All this time I've made excuses for you, accepted how you hated my sister with no good cause, but now? For a girl you purported to adore? You'd have her locked away in an asylum to go mad just to ease your groundless fears?"

Kate caught one of Lily's hands again and held it in a tight grip. "Mistress, you have a good heart, too good sometimes. You cannot see how the monsters are taking advantage of you. Everyone knows Naturals are dangerous. They only look like people. Inside, they're all done up in the devil's magic. Even your little sister. You see who she was before the devil in your bloodline woke up because you look with love. But there is nothing left of that person except a shell, the same shell born to hold evil. Surely you recognize the truth as much as you want to deny it. Why else would you have sent your sister away?"

Lily's eyes widened with surprise as she took in Kate's words and understood how the lady's maid had seen her choice. Lily's head started shaking before her dazed mind could catch up, her temper bursting free.

"You think you know everything. You think you understand, but you don't. I didn't send Sam away for our protection but for her own. Because of ignorant fools like you who make innocent Naturals into little more than hunted beasts then charge them with the crime of being what you've made them. You, and all those who think as you do, are the monsters."

She found the strength to rise, burning reserves she could ill afford to lose, but it didn't last.

While Bell continued working, oblivious to the battle going on beside her, Lily sank back onto the couch, exhausted.

Kate leapt up to grab an extra pillow from another chair, tucking it behind Lily's head as though they hadn't been arguing so fiercely only moments before.

"You mustn't wear yourself out any more than you already have. You are weak. All this has been too much for you."

Lily wanted to protest that she'd been stronger with Bell's company than in the past several years, but no words came. As much as she wanted to reject Kate's touch, she had no strength left. Inwardly, she might be seething, but there remained nothing to draw on.

"Hush, now. You mustn't get so agitated. You were never strong enough to do what was necessary. What was right. Bad enough your sister, but how could you find the strength should your whole line be tainted? If only you'd adopted a good child. I never would have guessed you'd go out and find a monster when I made sure you couldn't bring another into this world. Don't worry. We'll find you a child to dote on. One who deserves your love."

Lily stared up at the woman she'd thought she'd known, the one she'd considered ignorant but innocent of malice. The soothing tone continued to wash over her, clashing with hateful words.

Could the lady's maid have meant what she said? Had she been harming Lily this whole time, preventing her from bringing a child to term? This went so far beyond Kate's dislike of Naturals, Lily struggled to comprehend the condemning words. She found herself unable to fight the sensation of hatred flooding her veins with every stroke on her head, though it was meant to be comforting. She would have pulled away if she could have found the strength.

If ever the lady's maid held love for her, that twisted emotion bore little in common with true affection.

*H*ENRY FROZE WHERE HE STOOD at the parlor door after riding hard through the day, unable to believe what he'd heard.

His instincts about Lily's danger had been truer than he could have imagined, if much too late. He'd known Kate since she was a child and had never seen the evil that lurked behind her abrasive personality.

Blind rage swept over him as he strode through the open door, his heavy step drawing the attention of both women.

He met Lily's stricken gaze first, then turned on Kate and closed his hands around her arms with force.

"You have been poisoning my Lily. You've been killing her slowly, watching her weaken with every passing year, and yet you persisted." He shook Kate hard enough for her teeth to clack together. "She stood up for you. Even Sam took your side, thinking you good for her sister. Sam wouldn't have had to leave at all if not for your doing."

The magnitude of that struck him silent, but Kate made no effort to bridge the gap, staring at him with wide, fearful eyes.

His voice became quieter—tighter—as he continued, "You will be gone from this house this very night, or I will throw you out the door myself. If you ever think to speak ill of this household or anyone within it, I will charge you with attempting to murder the wife of a nobleman. Perhaps bloodline doesn't hold the weight it once did, but the House of Lords and the House of Commons are both too intelligent not to recognize the consequences if such a crime is left unpunished. I'll have many a doctor as witness, if only to show why they were unable to help Lily."

Kate paled beneath his glare, lighter than he'd ever seen her. His message had been heard.

Tears gathered in her eyes as she said, "I didn't poison her. I swear I did not. The midwife said it would loosen the child, and it did. I only gave her a little after that. To make sure no other rooted in her belly, nothing more. I did not cause her sickness. It's the poisons in her body, in her bloodline. The same devil as made a monster of her sister."

Henry blinked, stunned once again at her oblivion, and how easily she spoke of killing his child. How could this woman not see the connection between her crimes and Lily's persistent weakness?

"You might not have intended this, but only a fool would miss how she sickened from the moment you poisoned her. You killed her child—my child—and are trying to kill my wife. How could you have watched her struggle through all those visits to doctors who could do nothing and never once question the potion you gave her? She grew better as soon as you weren't here. I don't know how I failed to see that before. Did it not make you hesitate?"

He thrust her from him, the feel of her skin like boiling water poured over his palms. The pieces fell together in a lightning strike with that thought, only his ignorance keeping him blind before.

"The tea. She didn't drink your vile concoction, something she suffered only to make you feel as though you could help. You fed her the very poison that was killing her under the guise of a cure when no one beyond yourself knew what caused her to fade."

"But the midwife—"

Something drove Henry to continue. He needed to see comprehension of her crimes in Kate's expression.

"An imperfect understanding of herbs gathered based on what a midwife, if she were even that, said to use once? I wonder what fanciful tale you spun to get a goodly midwife to reveal even so much. When Lily grew ill, you should have stopped, though in truth, you should never have begun. You might have chosen not to see, but you are responsible in any case. Responsible for the loss of our child and Lily's poor health." His voice rose with every biting word. "Your blindness will weigh on your soul from this day forth. Even if your mistress recovers fully, as I suspect she will, you are the cause of her nearing death and of her greatest sorrow. Do not add more crimes to your ledger, or I will see you hang for them."

Kate gave a trembling nod, her lower lip trapped by her teeth, then she ran from the room toward the back of the manor and the servant quarters.

Henry sank into the nearest chair, one hand shading his face. An exhaustion to match Lily's crushed him. All this time, he'd been curling a viper to his chest, or worse, to Lily's own skin.

His wife had been strong as an ox when first they'd met, though she might not have appreciated the comparison. She'd faced everything life had to send at her and never held anything back. Her frail appearance served to throw people off guard, but it had never been more than skin deep until she married him.

He'd fought the belief his seed had caused her decline, but it had haunted him ever since they lost the child. The babe had gone before it made a noticeable impression on Lily's form. On his wife, though, he'd seen the marks cut deep.

They hadn't even mentioned it to Sam before fate ripped the child from their hearts. The loss thrust a deep sadness into Lily. A melancholy that took root and festered perhaps the worse for remaining unspoken.

From then, it was one sickness after another until she never quite regained her strength.

All this flashed through his mind, but with his new understanding, each moment became rewritten. Neither fate nor bad luck had destroyed his loving wife. His child had not been responsible. Worse, his child had been murdered.

He knew the magnitude of Kate's crimes would hit him fully later on, but for now, he had to focus on Lily. His wife's declining health had been the result of a deliberate act, and by the one he'd trusted to see to her care. The rally he'd thrilled in so recently had come only with the lady's maid sent to her father's house. And with Kate's return, that strength had drained away once more.

"She meant no harm."

He pivoted his head to stare at Lily with his mouth dropped open.

She waved a hand as though to soothe his unspoken protest. "I do not regret her dismissal. She could not stay here, not after what she's done, but don't let her failings weigh against you. You are not at fault. If any should be, I'm the one who defended her at every turn, who refused to recognize how the woman's dislike for Sam had festered into hatred. How could we see what she, herself, could not? In her own, twisted way, Kate thought she was doing what was right. And many an early babe is lost. She may not even have succeeded there."

A sigh rose from deep in his chest as Henry's gaze softened. "You are too kindhearted by far. It matters not what her motivations might have been. This is why I'm fighting Parliament after all. We've trained a nation to hate when that very hatred leads to criminal acts in the name of what is believed to be right. It's human nature to fear what we cannot understand. Civilization has moved us from that base nature, but has not removed it altogether." He managed a shaky smile as he stretched a hand out to lay hold of hers. "What matters is you will recover now, not for a short while, but for all time."

Lily chuckled at that, an unlikely response until she added, "I'm just happy to be done drinking that bitter tea."

22

*L*ily left Henry to watch Bell until the bout had ended while she saw to getting a meal prepared. He'd ridden hard to get here and not had the best of welcomes.

"Is it true, mistress," Abigail asked when she saw Lily heading for the kitchen.

The question reminded Lily of the bigger issue. Would any in the household trust her again knowing what she'd kept from them all?

The silence lay heavy between Abigail and Lily until it seemed too weighty to break, but no good would come of denying the truth now. She'd just have to suffer the consequences of her decision.

"Yes, Abby, it's true. Bell is as much a Natural as Sam ever was."

Whatever she'd expected, the confusion on the girl's face surprised her as did Abigail's quick gesture to wave the statement away.

"Not that, mistress, though it does seem they're drawn to you. No, is she finally gone for good? We heard that much in her mutters, but there's none as can quite believe it."

Lily could have laughed aloud in relief at the easy acceptance of Bell's knack. Instead, she frowned, chastising herself for not seeing it before.

"Will none of you miss her?"

Abigail grinned. "What's there to miss? She's thought herself better than us ever since you made her a lady's maid. Putting on airs, calling out orders, and talking mean about Miss Samantha when you couldn't hear. If not for how she made you happy, we'd have tossed her out ourselves long ago."

The maid gasped and slapped both hands over her mouth much too late to call back her words.

"Begging your pardon, mistress. Didn't mean a word of it." Abigail gave a clumsy curtsy and scrambled away toward the kitchen.

"Yes. She's really gone," Lily called after her, aware enough to recognize the others had sent Abigail to find out the truth. Another of the staff might have struggled for a safe way to frame the question. Abigail could be counted on to speak without hesitation or thought.

Lily followed at a slower pace, stunned at how little she'd noticed. Kate might have been blind to the effects her medicine had—though preventing an heir should have been crime enough—but how could Lily have failed to see to how the whole household saw the lady's maid?

Her mind opened up the painful moment when she learned what the woman she'd come to trust felt about her very own sister, and Lily sighed. She'd been so happy here that she'd seen the same in the faces of all around her. Instinct made her withhold Bell's talents when they first met, knowing Kate had to love the girl before she learned the truth, but that had not been enough to warn her.

The door to the kitchen gave way with a slight push, and the manor staff pivoted to stare at Lily. Every member had gathered here except Kate. Even the stable boys laid claim to a corner of the table.

The air took on an expectant nature. Perhaps Abigail's account had not been any more believable than Kate's mutters.

A smile twitched her mouth as Lily realized the right thing to say. "All concerns about my health are now relieved."

Before any of the others could react, Cook snapped out, "It were the tea. I knew it."

That brought a babble of cries and questions from the others, but over it all, Lily met Cook's gaze and gave a firm nod.

The woman who had adored Sam as though her own kin brushed the others aside as she marched to where the tea chest stood, the key for same held only by her and Kate.

"I'll be washing these down the river. Only way to be sure they'll never harm another soul. I always knew that girl was up to no good the way she kept me from the tea chest all times."

Lily swallowed back her request for a meal, unwilling to delay the disposal of those poisons another moment. The manor would soon be washed free of the taint.

Another smile teased as her arm curled around a belly she'd long thought barren. Perhaps more than just her strength would heal.

"Is it true the little tot has talent?" One of the stable boys asked in his usual forward manner.

"That part is true as well."

She searched each expression for any sign of Kate's hatred and could find none.

Not all were happy with this revelation, knowing the risks that came from harboring a fugitive as much as fearing a Natural losing control, but even the furrowed brows held smiles beneath them.

"Can she make me a horse like she did Ben?" the second stable boy said with a nudge to the first, revealing Lily's present had not been the only one before Bell promised to stop.

A laugh burst from Lily. "I don't know, but you can ask."

Maybe she wouldn't turn Bell fearful in keeping her here after all.

With Kate gone, it seemed the good will Bell had earned when just a little girl stayed strong. For all the complications Bell brought with her, the staff proved no less welcoming of a fugitive Natural than they'd been of an orphan.

Overwhelmed by their goodness, Lily almost forgot what had brought her here in the first place. Only Cook's return with a satisfied grin on her red and sweating features reminded Lily of her purpose.

"When you've had a chance to catch your breath, the master would appreciate an early dinner before the sun goes down. He arrived just recently and had only a quick meal on the journey."

She added the last when Cook's expression turned to consternation. Apparently Kate had not revealed his arrival, though from how the woman turned to glare at the stable boys, they should have shared this information as well.

"I'll get something going this very minute, mistress. It's good to have the master home."

"Shall I set you up for the night?"

Abigail's question confused Lily until she realized what it meant. "Yes, Abby, please do. Though I suspect I won't be retiring as early for many years to come."

With that, she turned and left the kitchen to learn the state of her husband and their fosterling Natural. She almost didn't know how to feel without the weight of her impending demise hanging over her.

If only she could tell Sam.

23

Henry smiled grimly as he strode past the parlor and headed for his study. Two days since he'd sent Kate packing, and already the household sang with good cheer. He knew the signs of Lily's early recovery held as much responsibility as Kate's absence, but though he happily celebrated her return to health, a permanent one this time, worry kept him tense.

Lily had said Kate meant to help them. She understood what had driven the maid even though that motivation meant destroying their first child and preventing any after.

He didn't argue since the idea seemed to offer her comfort, but it lingered in his mind until he could no longer avoid the truth.

The desk chair creaked as he sank into it and dropped his head to rest on tented arms.

If Kate thought she'd been helping, rather than being cowed by her discovery, what would stop her from feeling just as betrayed as they were? What hold had they on her, or any of the manor, beyond loyalty?

His threats became empty when measured against what the former lady's maid knew.

She could just as easily turn on them and level charges of harboring a fugitive Natural, accusations that would stand all the firmer for his efforts to bring about changes in the legal status of those with such a rare talent.

He could not lay his hopes on her good nature, either. She might not have realized how she caused Lily's decline, but neither did that ignorance make her innocent. She had chosen to kill their child, had knowingly prevented any other from taking root. Her love for Lily, if she still held any, would not be stronger than her hatred of Naturals for all they'd done her little harm. It had not been strong enough to allow her beloved mistress to carry a child.

"What has you so worried?" Lily asked from the doorway, bringing Henry's head up.

Framed there with the early morning light around her, she looked lovelier than he'd ever seen her. She held herself with a strength that had been lacking all too often in the past years. Though a full recovery would take time, the difference without a nightly dose of poison was marked.

Henry took in the sight of her and understood the message behind her strength. He could not keep her in ignorance, not of his concerns nor of the only solution he could see.

"I ride for London tonight. Parson will stand before Parliament tomorrow evening, and I will be there at his side."

She nodded, knowing well enough his time at the manor had been limited.

"What if Kate comes back with me gone? What if she brings the constables?"

Lily crossed to his side, placing one hand on his shoulder. "She wouldn't do such a thing, if not out of love for me and regret for what she's done, then out of fear of the consequences."

He twisted to face her, catching her hands in his. "Who will believe us when we're brought up on charges of harboring fugitive Naturals? Who could we call on to testify against her when an accidental word from any of the manor staff would condemn us and them right alongside?"

Her smile dropped away, and he wished he hadn't been responsible for the loss.

"What are we to do then? Go into hiding? Prove ourselves wrong by attempting an escape?"

He pulled her toward him so she could settle on his lap, his arms embracing her.

"I must leave for London. I cannot falter in what I've started, not for the sake of all Naturals, nor for our own. But neither can we sit back and hope Kate will do nothing. The longer she remains, the greater the risk becomes."

Her head leaned on his chest, but Lily's words came clearly. "Would you have her deported then? Cast out for doing what she believed, what all the country believes, is right?"

He shook his head. "Not all the country, but enough. For her to stand trial would be as much a risk as having her wandering free. I was thinking more the time has come to do the Grand Tour we'd promised once your health returned."

Lily pulled away, her smile restored. "To the Continent? To find Sam?"

He cursed the fate that made him strip her joy away. "And to deliver Bell."

She fell silent, so still against him he could feel her heart beat like a moth trapped in an oil lamp.

"She cannot stay here, Lily. Surely you can see that. For all we enjoy her company, her presence threatens everyone, and more so with Kate running free. The constables might not believe her word alone, but if she could show them a real Natural? Bell might not have fallen so easily into a bout as Sam did, but the risk is all too real."

"Hush," Lily said, pressing her palms to his chest. "Be quiet a moment longer."

He pulled her close, hugging her to him as tight as he could manage without crushing her.

How long they stayed so, he could not have said, but when the clock on the shelf behind him struck out the half hour, she pulled away, wiping furtively at tears spilling down her cheeks.

He didn't hold her back when she stood.

"Well, that's that then. I'll go prepare Bell for her grand adventure off to the safe haven. At least this time I can travel at her side."

Henry admired the strength Lily claimed more than ever for how her tones came out even and cheerful. No need for Bell to learn how much this decision tore them apart. It would be hard enough on her having been raised with the idea she could live here in England in safety.

"You have some time to prepare," he said before Lily could step past the door. "Parson must speak first, and then I will announce my pending absence. I'll think of something that will hold up to scrutiny. With Bell in safety, it would be our word against that of a woman dismissed for grave misbehavior even if we keep the specifics of her crime unspoken. Kate won't speak or she'll be punished alongside us for harboring a Natural."

He waited for Lily to say something, but she did not defend or condemn her former lady's maid.

"It will be three days at most before I can return. Enjoy what time you have with Bell."

A strangled laugh escaped his wife at the last. "You think a Grand Tour something one can put together in a matter of hours?"

That brought the first true smile of the day to his lips. "I know you well enough to be sure if any could do this, you will. Go on now. I'll write to my man in Dover. He'll secure passage for us in four days' time, so be ready."

24

W hen Lily woke, warmth at her side made her forget
Henry had left the night before. Instead, Bell had
joined her once again. The little girl had seemed oblivious in
her bout while the world around her changed, but she'd returned to the nervous child Lily had found at the workshop,
perhaps more for having failed to retain control than because
of Kate's treachery.

A quick cuddle brought Bell awake with a smile, one Lily
struggled to return.

"What will we do today?" Bell asked, rubbing the sleep
from her eyes.

The question froze Lily as she realized how much stronger
she felt already. Kate's poisons must not have had long enough
to take root without constant reinforcement after Lily had
cleared her system during the time of Kate's earlier banishment.

She laughed, the wonder only reaching her now, with the
harsh decisions beyond them.

"We can do whatever you desire, Bell."

The little girl's shout of delight drowned out Lily's sigh
when she realized the decision might be made, but she had yet
to explain what they had to do.

She swung out of bed, determined to enjoy the day without letting what was to come hang over her. Tonight would be
soon enough to inform Bell of the plan to take her to the

Continent. Maybe by then it wouldn't feel as much like abandonment.

"Can we go on a picnic again? And take Sunshine? I know where the leash is."

Bell stopped talking all of a sudden, her tension showing she'd understood enough of what had happened three days earlier to know everything had changed, if not during her bout then because of the servants gossiping.

"Yes," Lily said, ignoring the pause. "We can take Sunshine on his leash. A picnic should do both of us some good."

Why she chose the direction she did when they set out later, burdened with an overflowing basket, a blanket, and of course, the kitten, she couldn't have said. The tree they chose for shade stood tall and welcoming with big roots to use as benches even. The grass rustled in the wind, and wild flowers grew in abundance.

They'd never come here before for one simple reason: it overlooked Sam's workshop.

Lily tried to ignore the structure, and in all honesty, Bell did not seem to notice it at all, but Lily knew where it stood no matter which direction she looked.

The workshop had been Sam's pride and joy. She'd been so happy when Henry gave her the space on her tenth birthday. She'd practically glowed with it.

When Sam prepared to leave, though, Lily knew each time her sister went out to the workshop from the drag in her step and the heaviness that seemed to have settled on her shoulders.

The workshop, too, had been instrumental in bringing Bell to them. It had drawn her to the manor, and the mechanicals trapped within had been noisy enough to wake Lily before Bell could free them.

"Come here, Lily. Come."

She shook off her thoughts and rose to answer Bell's call, expecting a crown of flowers for her hair.

Instead, the girl pointed to a patch of wild strawberries.

"Can we pick them? They taste so wonderful. We could bring some back for the rest."

Lily smiled at Bell, amazed again at how she thought of others before herself even when she'd been cast out under the threat of imprisonment. How many times had she come across a patch like this and it had become her first meal in days?

"Of course we can. Do leave some for the birds, though. I have just the thing for it in the basket."

She walked to the tree and dug out a linen-wrapped package of sweet pastries made, most likely, from other wild strawberry patches.

"We'll have to empty it first," she told Bell with a laugh, dropping to sit at the little girl's side.

Bell did not argue as she set to work devouring the treat Cook had left her. She might not have Sam's hearty appetite, but who could resist such delights?

Lily's gaze wandered as she nibbled until once again it rested on the firm wood walls of the workshop. From here, she could not see the complicated mechanism that sealed the door, but she knew it was there. That contraption, more than any other, reminded Lily of what it meant to be a Natural in England where your very existence endangered all those around you.

A sigh slipped out as she realized she could not pretend any longer.

"Bell?"

The little girl twisted to face her, a smile on lips that soon lost their curve when her gaze crossed Lily's. "What is it? Are you feeling ill?"

Lily shook her head. "No, I'm not ill. I'm better than I have been in a long time. It's not that."

Her words dried up as she struggled for a way to explain that wouldn't sound like they didn't want Bell anymore.

Bell put a small hand on Lily's knee. "Then it's about me leaving." She shrugged. "I heard you and Henry speaking of it."

Lily pulled Bell into her arms, ignoring the little girl's sticky fingers and berry-stained lips. "It's not that we want you to go. You must know that. It's for your safety as much as ours."

Bell pulled back to give a solemn nod. "I do know. It's like when my parents sent me off. I've loved this time with you, but I always knew it would come to an end."

She rose, her shoulders slumped and hands twisted together.

"Can I pack a few of the things you've given me? Like the dresses?" Bell pinched some of the fabric between two fingers and lifted it as if to explain what she meant. "I didn't have time before."

Lily stared, shocked.

In all her thinking on how to tell, she'd never imagined Bell would have realized or learned on her own. Nor how it would seem the same as when she left her first home.

"Of course you can take them. All of them. They are yours."

Bell gave a weak smile. "You and Henry have been very generous. I don't think I can carry so much."

The last comment brought together what Bell had said to form a very different picture.

"Wait." Lily put out a hand to catch Bell as the little girl turned to head back to the manor that very moment. "You may have listened at the door, but you didn't stay long enough to hear the full of it."

She swallowed a comment about those who overhear, stunned by the hope that sparked in Bell's eyes, a hope she could not fulfill.

"You do have to leave, Bell. We cannot chance Kate reporting you to the authorities. You'd never survive how they treat Naturals. But you won't have to carry your things. Henry will take care of that. We will be going together. The three of us, and Abby even. We'll take you to a safe place on the Continent where you can live with others like you."

"Did Sam go there?"

From Bell's excitement, Lily could tell she'd longed to meet someone like her for a while, but the question made Lily drop her gaze to interlaced fingers.

"I hope so, Bell. Truly I do."

"Then it'll be a grand adventure. Come, Lily. We have much to prepare."

The girl's eagerness broke through the touch of melancholy that had overcome Lily at the thought of her sister. Instead, she laughed.

"What about the berries?"

Bell grinned as she tugged Lily's hand to make her rise. "The birds can feast on them."

25

enry arrived in London late enough the previous day, or should he say early enough this morning, to not only succeed in overcoming any inclination to country hours but to sleep in late even for the city folk. Still, he had time for a leisurely midday meal before making his way to the Palace of Westminster in time for the full session.

The actual time of Parson's audience remained unknown to him, but he wanted the members to see how he took the rest of the issues seriously as well. No one would listen to him if they felt he came only to serve his own purpose and ignore the interests of others. Not that he could blame them. The Houses were supposed to speak for the country as a whole, not a single man's pleasure no matter how important the cause.

The seats were already crowded by the time he made his appearance. Unless they had some other big debate scheduled, this showed strong interest in his purpose, though whether for or against it remained to be seen. The question left him antsy, and despite his best efforts, he had a hard time focusing on the minor concerns and grievances raised.

It appeared he was not the only one as the Lord Chancellor seemed a bit testy when he announced Parson. Henry had not been given the right to question the officer. That fell to one of the men standing firmly in the against category. Perhaps the assignment should have worried Henry, but he knew Parson too well to think he'd be rattled by any man, much less one trying to make him trip over his own feet.

"So, in your duties as a police officer, have you ever come across a Natural just out to help people?"

Henry's thoughts had started to wander but snapped back into focus with the question.

The look of patent disbelief Parson leveled on the other man sent ripples of shocked laughter through the members.

"Are you in the habit of calling up the police to prevent a helpful sort, then?" Parson asked, emphasizing his brogue and provoking another round of laughter. "But assuming you didn't mean such actions should be stopped by force if necessary, I'd have to say no, and grateful I am for it. The law is clear. It makes no distinction between the helpful and harmful in the case of Naturals. Certainly I avoid going out seeking those as do not make a nuisance, if not an outright danger, of themselves. If so, I'd have no choice but to incarcerate them for life. Seems a hefty punishment for being what you were born to be, wouldn't you think?"

The questioning continued, but with every attempt countered in such a way to keep the members on Parson's side. The police officer emphasized again and again the need to capture the criminals but leave those not so inclined to live their lives in peace. Henry had not doubted his friend's ability to handle this delicate task, but could see a growing frustration among those opposing him. They'd thought to make good use of a simple police officer, a plan that spoke poorly of their opinion of those who upheld the very laws they sought to defend.

Their ignorance had played right into Henry's hand. After this, he doubted many would stand undecided.

Tension swept his form as he realized the danger in having made a fool of his opponents. They'd have to work harder to dismiss him. An upstanding man as he appeared to be would have nothing to fear, but they had only to startle Bell and everything could be torn apart.

"Lord Stapleton, if you please. Have you anything to add to this account?"

Henry turned to face the Lord Chancellor, unprepared for once, but still he pushed to his feet.

"I have nothing much to add to the officer's account, having told you of my experiences before. However, I would like to inform you all that I will be absent for a while. I have learned from my inquiries the orphan child my wife and I have adopted may, in fact, have relatives still living in Spain. We will be taking her to the Continent as it's only right to restore her to family should she have some."

He thought to sit down as soon as he finished speaking, having planned to deliver the information via letter before given the chance to present it here, but then hesitated.

"Because the laws are different among the continental countries, I may have the opportunity to observe Naturals living under lesser restrictions and without the threat of retribution tied to their very existence. I will attempt to ensure this so I can report back on their ability to contribute to those societies."

Lord Vereham, who had questioned Parson, jerked to his feet as well. "You are hardly an unbiased observer."

The Lord Chancellor called for order to rebuke the interruption, but Lord Vereham settled without protest, having made his point.

Henry gave a half salute in the man's direction. "While I don't agree with your objection, I'd be happy to include additional volunteers should they want to accompany me."

He tried not to look concerned as he waited for a response, hoping only such an undertaking would have little appeal with the approaching summer warmth. Whether landholders or merchants, good weather should not be wasted and few had such trustworthy staff to manage an unexpected absence. Even more, his opponents would want to go on their own to make up tales. To see the reality with others meant being caught in a bald-faced lie if they did speak a tale over what they'd observed.

The silence ran long enough for there to be no question. Henry did not press this issue, nor did he release the sigh of relief he truly felt. To hide Bell's abilities from others should be easy enough when she'd amply demonstrated her control, but the journey would have its own complications. How they would have released her to live in a safe haven while keeping their companions ignorant of just where she'd gone, he did not know.

"Should you decide to put together a safe passage for a functioning Natural, my man Stuart in Dover will be able to get it to me promptly. I should then endeavor to return with a free Natural willing to demonstrate all they have to offer to those interested in exploring this avenue further. If not, you'll at least have my accounts to consider."

With that, he sank to his seat, struggling to keep his knees from shaking.

His family had done much over the generations that required living double lives to help those in need. He'd never thought to do so himself, though, preferring a more direct role as a police officer. He'd found the deceit much easier out on the manor where engagements were limited. Still, he would not have given up his time with Sam for anything, nor would he see Bell mistreated. A little subterfuge on his part seemed a paltry price to pay.

As soon as he returned to his London town house, he'd write Lily a letter describing the announcement in such a way so she would understand the plan and ensure both she and Bell said nothing to raise questions. He had things to arrange here in London, but would soon be headed back to his family and then on to the Continent.

THERE HAD BEEN NO LACK of tears when Lily explained their plans the night before. She had told only the simple truth when she said much had to be done to prepare for a Grand Tour.

The staff's reaction, from Cook down to the youngest stable boy, only showed their warm hearts. Though orphaned and a Natural, they'd taken to Bell as one of the family and would miss her sorely. Still, they dove into the preparations without hesitation.

For the longest while, Lily had little time to think, which she could only consider a blessing. She'd already suffered the loss of her sister who had been all but a child of her body. Now, she would once again suffer as Bell left her.

Despite all the distractions, though, something chewed at the back of Lily's mind, keeping her anxious even when she had all the help she could have asked for. They were on schedule to leave for Dover when Henry returned from London at least.

Everyone else sought their beds at the end of the busy day with happy relief, but Lily lay there in the darkness, Bell nestled against her side, and stared at the ceiling, unable to sleep.

The wind rustled through the branches of a tree outside her window, the leaves sounding like little feet scampering across the floor.

Lily sat bolt upright, almost waking Bell from her deep sleep.

As she had what seemed a lifetime ago, she slipped from her bed with only one destination mind. She did stop to put on slippers this time, remembering the cuts in her feet from going barefoot.

She soon came to a halt in front of Sam's workshop, her mind flooded with memories of discovering Bell, and even before then, of Sam chattering on about her latest creation.

The wood felt warm beneath her fingers as if alive, and alive it was in part. Alive with possibilities, none of which would do aught but harm.

She could take Bell to the Continent as she'd sent Sam, and even prevent the birth of her own child if Kate were to be believed in thinking Naturals had ties to a bloodline. None of that would do the least bit of good if someone were to come investigating Kate's claims.

They had only to open this workshop, and they'd know the truth. They would tear Henry's property apart looking for Naturals who no longer existed here. Even without a Natural in person, the workshop offered damning evidence enough to charge Henry with a crime against country and destroy the family name he was so proud of. His title would be stricken from the ranks of peerage, and his family name cursed. His efforts to overturn the Natural laws would crumble, and Parliament might even strengthen the penalties in response to Henry's deceit.

All because of her.

Before she could hesitate a moment longer, Lily released the lock Sam had built to secure the workshop, her hands trembling. She stepped back as soon as the door swung wide, half expecting the machines to attack her for leaving them trapped, for keeping them from Sam.

Nothing happened.

The workshop showed no signs of life at all. She viewed only a jumble of machines and parts crammed into a space almost too small to hold them, too mixed together to be clear as to form or function. She had not expected anything like this, especially when the mechanicals had been able to speak to Bell not so long ago.

Her fear dissipated as she stared at all that remained of her little sister's time on the estate.

Sam had been so proud of her creations, so happy to have helped them become what they desired, and yet, it all came down to this. Her sister lost and the machines struck lifeless in her absence.

Tears threatened to flood Lily's eyes, as much for the pending loss of Bell as the loss she'd already suffered.

She should be grateful these mechanisms no longer bore the shape they'd been given. That they no longer proclaimed the truth far and wide. Instead, they became one more betrayal. One more way Sam was lost to her.

"Is this all she meant to you? Would you give up so easily?" The tears dried as anger took their place though she had little reason to suppose the machines could even hear her. "Sam would never have given up on you. She locked you in here to keep you safe, not to cast you aside. It would hurt her to know you'd forgotten what she gave you."

Though the mechanisms had not moved, a weird tension filled the air. Lily had the sense they were listening, waiting for her to say something more, to give them direction.

She laughed, a sour, bitter sound. She'd made them back into what they'd been from the start—a danger to Henry and everyone who lived on the estate.

"You have to go. You have to scatter far from here as you can manage. Sam wouldn't have wanted harm to come to her family, and you pose a far greater danger than she could have imagined. Get on with you."

Lily paused, her chest tight with what she wanted to say for all she knew she should not.

And still they waited.

She drew in a deep breath and let it out slowly.

What difference would it make? Sam had gone to the Continent or been captured despite word not reaching them. Otherwise, she would've returned home no matter the risk.

Lily's eyes fell closed for only a heartbeat before she stared at the collection of machinery, lit by the streaming moonlight.

"Go find Sam wherever she is. Help my little sister."

The words barely had the strength to reach her own ears, but that wish, that desire, provoked the expected reaction.

One after another, the mechanisms broke free of their tangle and crept or lurched out of the workshop, moving slowly as though their joints had stiffened with age. More and more came, the sheer number stunning Lily to silence, but soon they were all gone, striking out in every possible direction, cast to the winds.

She stared after the last for as long as she could until shadow hid even the glint of moonlight on metal.

Only Henry's pocket watch remained to condemn them, and its fortitude had been proved time and again, between all their trips to Dover and his days spent in London, with no one the wiser to its presence.

Lily should have been glad, or even relieved, to have them gone. She should have considered the matter settled.

Instead, she stared across the fields, sending her hopes when her eyes could no longer make out their presence. If Sam were somehow still in England, Lily wanted the machines to find her little sister, to free Sam from whoever held her captive even if she could no longer come home. And if they found no sign of her, then let Lily herself learn the truth when she discovered Sam healthy and happy in the safe haven after all.

Thank You for Reading

I hope you enjoyed *Life and Law*, and the start of Henry and Lily's adventures. They have much to experience before they join Sam and Nat in later tales. I'd appreciate an honest review at your favorite store and/or wherever you go to learn about books. Your feedback will help The Steamship Chronicles find the right audience.

I'd love to hear what you think of my stories by email at author@margaretmcgaffeyfisk.com or drop by my website at margaretmcgaffeyfisk.com.

If you sign up for my monthly newsletter, I'll share a bit of my writing and publishing journey, fun events, and even snippets or pre-publication stories as a thank you for letting me into your inbox. You can also choose to receive release announcements, which are split into genre and go out only when a new title is available in that genre. Feel free to select as many options as you'd like.

If you'd like to read an excerpt from *Steam and Shadows*, please turn the page.

Excerpt

Steam and Shadows
Book Five of The Steamship Chronicles

*Henry and Lily take Bell to the Continent in search of the safe haven
and are delighted at the differences, but sometimes things are not as they
appear.*

When at last their chance came, Henry and Lily struggled to keep up as Bell raced down the ship's gangplank onto the foreign shore. No one seeing her now would
believe her ladylike behavior at the manor. Not that he could
blame the little girl.

They stepped off into a wonderland of mechanical devices
in every direction. Some of the sellers displayed mechanisms
for performing simple tasks from kneading dough to turning
pages of musical notation when playing the pianoforte. A
track much like those used by the railroads displayed how
small wagons could bring food fresh from the kitchen into the
dining room where it could be served. He even saw a device
that could replace a lady's maid for the task of brushing hair.

"Isn't it wonderful?" Bell asked as she tugged them down a second row. "Have you ever seen such amazing things?"

Henry exchanged a look with Lily, sure his wife was searching for the same signs as he sought, but Bell did not seem affected at all. So many devices, and the young Natural showed no interest in changing or transforming any of them.

They rounded a corner and came to an open space filled with people of all ages, some sitting in the dirt and others standing at the edges.

A tone rang out from a hidden bell, and all conversation ceased. Young and old alike looked toward the far side as if straining to hear something not yet said.

"It's a puppet show." Bell's exclamation seemed all too loud in the expectant silence, and more than a few of those gathered turned to glare at her.

Henry's instincts told him to hide her away. They could not afford to bring attention to themselves, and especially not to Bell.

Before he could act, though, with a clatter and a rustle, the curtains parted. What had been hidden behind entranced him as much as any others.

It was not a puppet show, or at least nothing like the puppet shows he had seen. He had heard tales of similar performances at the king's palace many years ago with strings to guide and ropes to pull. These actors had none.

Every one was a different mechanical person. The scenes behind them changed from one moment to the next as a different piece slid into place without a sound. They spoke no more than puppets would, but their movements were so lifelike with no evidence of guides. Henry knew he was in the presence of a Natural's work.

The story told in pantomime no longer had any power to hold his attention. He looked from audience member to audience member, and not a one showed any sign of fear or anger. For all that they'd been seeking a safe haven, for all he knew the laws toward Naturals were different here on the continent, until this very moment, he had not truly believed they could be.

He reached out to draw his family in close, not to protect them, but to share in the joy of his discovery. Whether they understood what he'd seen or not, this simple performance proved Naturals were considered no different than any other type of skilled person. All of the mechanisms they'd admired up to this point could have been created by a craftsman, but not this. He knew of only one type of skilled person who could create self-locomoting mechanical devices, yet here the people sat, as though they enjoyed the work of a farmer, woodcarver, or blacksmith.

Learn more about *Steam and Shadows*
on margaretmcgaffeyfisk.com.

About the Author

Margaret McGaffey Fisk is a story-teller who explores tales across genres and worlds. Raised in the Foreign Service where she developed a love for anthropology, she has been a data entry clerk, veterinary tech, editor, support engineer, and programmer, among other roles. She pulls on her studies and experiences to give depth to the cultures and people that form the heart of her stories. As her website is titled, she offers tales to tide you over.

She'd love to hear from you through any of the contact points or social media accounts listed on her website, or you can subscribe to one of her newsletters for release announcements, snippets, and other news:

margaretmcgaffeyfisk.com/subscribe-to-my-newsletter/

Website
MargaretMcGaffeyFisk.com

Acknowledgments

Life and Law starts the second volume of The Steamship Chronicles, and opens a new, but related, story in the same world. There are grand moments still to come, and much enjoyment to be had with Henry and Lily as well as Sam and Nat.

While this volume did not exist in the original idea, David Bridger is still responsible for getting me to play in the complicated world Sam inhabits. Along with David, I've had the support of my immediate and extended family on various aspects of this work, especially their patience. My husband Colin continues to fill in wherever I need him whether editing, cover consult, titles, plotting questions, or what have you. I know I can come to him for feedback, and he'll be happy to weigh in with an honest opinion or two. My sons have also been resources for both encouragement and specific feedback, especially when I'm wavering. Without them, from as early as the age of three on plot walks, I would not be the writer I am now.

My parents and sisters are endlessly patient as well, listening to book blurbs, editing pieces, or peering at cover art to identify where I might have slipped up. They push me to be better and to make what I put out in the world stronger.

To keep me honest, I am part of several writers' groups, with Dawn Hebein and Erin M. Hartshorn making direct contributions to *Life and Law*.

Once again, though, it is my readers who make this journey possible. I appreciate your eagerness for the next book in the series. Thank you for taking a chance on me and enjoying the experience enough to continue to walk this path at my side.

www.ingramcontent.com/pod-product-compliance
Lightning Source LLC
Chambersburg PA
CBHW030626120726
47904CB00006B/2046